TWICEBORN

SIX STORIES FROM THE FUTURE

C. L. KAGMI

INTRODUCTION

I did not set out to write a book about rebirth. It wasn't until I had these stories assembled that I noticed this common theme. Every single one of these stories centers on a character who is somehow born twice—once into ordinary human life, and then again into a new way of being that their old selves would be unable to understand.

A second, less exciting theme of this collection is that of moral questions. Always, one thing must be sacrificed to gain another. Is the murder of an innocent justified if it ensures the survival of a sentient species? How much voluntary risk is an acceptable price for progress? If you were an alien, would you give humanity lifesaving tech that they could then use against you?

My way of tackling these questions is old-school. I grew up reading Asimov and Auel, Bear and Butler, Clarke and Connie Willis. You won't find many action sequences or fight scenes in these pages. You won't find dystopias either.

I'm of the opinion that the most important battles are those fought inside of hearts and minds among people who are trying their best, and those are the battles we'll see here.

Many of these questions we are already grappling with in our world, whether we realize it or not.

Don't get me wrong. There *will* be aliens and genetic engineering and virtual worlds, too. I've been told that some of the aliens and AIs are kind of hot. And there will be murder. Kind of a lot of murder, actually.

Some of the contents here may disturb you. I have sometimes stumbled into the territory of horror by designing something scientifically which turns out to be rather offensive to typical human sensibilities. Some people like that. I hope you will.

I also hope to leave you just a little bit uncertain. The questions here are not easy, and I expect readers to be split in who they side with.

That, after all, is the point. If these questions were easy, they wouldn't be worth talking about.

TWICEBORN

"Twiceborn" first appeared in Issue 2 of *Compelling Science Fiction* in June of 2016. It was translated into Vietnamese by the illustrious Long Nguyễn for the Vietnamese fanzine SFVN. Devi Amar will appear in a new story in *Analog Science Fiction and Fact* in late 2021.

She will remember three suns.

The first will tell of her heritage; a scorching spark in a blue-violet sky, sharp black shadows cast on sea.

The second will tell her of her enemy, a yellow-white ball circling over human cities.

The third will show her where she must survive, a bloated ruby disk rising over a desolate waste.

It is too much to give a newborn, Jackson knows; on Homeworld, these memories would have unfurled slowly across the course of years. It is the defining gift of his species, to encode memory in molecules to direct the growth of a budding brain. And on Homeworld, they had *time.* Here, he does not.

It is one of the gifts the humans never learned. On Homeworld, they would have—

But Homeworld is no more, and he has perhaps three days before the humans find him and his newborn child. The infant brain will have to learn quickly, unfurling memories too fast, if she is to survive. If they are found before she is ready, he'll kill her himself to protect the others.

Learn fast, little one.

He watches the small human form as she lies sprawled in the low light of the desert cave. Jackson has removed the helmet of her pressure suit, for he does not share the humans' feigned concern for the natal ecosystem of this world. She can breathe the air; the helmets are to keep her microbes *in.* Still, the little girl's chest rises and falls in rapid bursts, mouth puffing with the effort of a new skill.

Learn fast.

The host body was seven, in Earth years. It takes Bharatha only eighty-one days to make a revolution around its red dwarf sun, but the humans still count by Earth's seasons. Why should they adapt to this planet? They will adapt this planet to themselves after they have learned what they want from its life. Or sooner, if its life is dangerous.

Jackson feels his lip curl. Thinks of all the things humans *didn't* learn from Homeworld before they fled and torched it. They had thought his people mindless parasites, an infection spreading through the water. How much they lost in their haste. How much they destroyed without remorse.

His people had made mistakes with their first human hosts, to be sure. They had not known how to manage the alien biochemistry, let alone how to stand, how to speak—or that the humans would kill them when they failed to conform.

To be fair, they had not realized that the humans were intelligent, either. They'd looked like so many mindless fish.

Jackson draws upon a human memory, a concept acquired from his host, a word—*'vampire.'*

A demon-possessed corpse, originally. A creature that put itself in your body, and took you out. The humans had known nothing of neurology then, but they knew they were not always in control of themselves.

The term seems appropriate for Jackson and his brood.

This little girl was seven, and so promising. That is why he picked her. She will be well-loved by those most dangerous to her, and her success in everything she does will come as no surprise.

Jackson sighs at the irony—that on this little world, the human rite of *Upanayanam* has become a true rebirth for some. A little girl and her parents came out here with him, for the ceremonial coming-of-age tour of their adopted planet. Something—*someone*—not human will return.

The girl's body spasms in a seizure. That is a good sign. It means his child, one of a precious few seeds he has planted to save his people, is integrating with the human brain. When the storm of electrical activity dies down, unless he's made some crucial error, the child will sit up.

To run, to hide, to always conceal herself—this is the burden he confers with life. The humans would raze this world, too, like Homeworld, like their own colony of Enlil, if they knew anything from Homeworld had survived. So she will have to be very careful. They all will.

It's a shame, Jackson thinks, that first contact went so poorly. If it had gone differently—

He turns his mind away from the unbearable pain of what *might* have been, from the unfathomable loss of the World-Minds and their uncounted billion agents. Keeps his thoughts carefully light: to what their peoples may have learned from each other, if they had not been so quick to bite.

He has learned from them because he has no choice. They will never learn from him, now; he cannot afford to teach them. Let the loss be theirs, then. And the gain his.

Life on dry land is something he's been forced to learn from them. Memories of an endless sapphire ocean, alive with chemical chatter, he must keep distant. Spaceflight, fire, more gifts from humanity to the ones they tried to eradicate. Speaking by shaping vibrations in the air instead of chemical chains.

"Jackson" is as good a name as any for him to use among the humans. It was his host's name, once. His *true* name is a tailored molecule, one only his kind can taste. A name that will be on his daughter's tongue when she is born.

"He" is his host's pronoun, too. His people had found gender in their lower hosts and discarded it as useless—but they had never encountered it in intelligent life before humanity. There are some interesting things, he has decided, about gender.

If nothing else, he needs to understand it to survive. So does she. He's done his best to include what teachings he can in the package he lovingly wrapped inside her cells. A thing their ancestors never needed, but they need it now.

The newborn shudders, moans. Strong enough now to follow programming he stored within her egg. She sits up. Jackson lets out a breath he hadn't realized he was holding.

Wide green eyes, the color of Bharatha's sky, blink at him from a dark brown face. He tells himself he did not choose the host for her eyes, but for her family and her aptitude. He tells himself this, but still the eyes are striking. They set her apart. That will be useful, later.

The newborn is afraid and confused. She has information and no context for it, a litany of facts and experiences and only a few minutes' acquaintance with consciousness. She is doing better than the last one. Perhaps he is learning how to teach.

"Shh," Jackson hushes her. If the two of them were human he'd hold her, but his people never did that. If they were on Homeworld he would release messages of love and care into the water for her to taste, but he can't do that here.

Better that she start off learning human symbols, anyway. Human *speech*.

"Shh," he says again. "Can you speak?"

An awkward, strangled squawk from the girls' larynx. It's something.

"Repeat after me," he says. "Aaaah. Ooooh."

He has three days to teach her to talk.

Miraculously, the girl is ready. Tears fill Jackson's eyes as he watches her—tears of pride. He preserved most of his host's emotional responses to help him blend in; sometimes, he is glad of this.

He has found a way to preserve his memories of his people. A way to recreate, someday, what was lost.

The child's memories have unfurled enough for her to pass as human, and to know that she is not. More memories will come to her in her dreams—dreams enough to last her centuries. And she might have that much time. Shortly after puberty, they will teach her how to tidy up the human epigenome and control the aging process of her body's cells.

She sits beside him now, illuminated in a shaft of scarlet sunlight that pours in from the mouth of the cave. Her mouth working, limbs fidgeting as she learns her motor connections. She raises fingers to touch her own face.

Jackson remembers the alien sensation, the first time he

touched his own. Skin that was warm and oh so dry, textured with hairs so fine the humans ceased to notice them. Fingers with bones in them like sticks to maintain form out of water; none of the nuance of pure-muscle limbs he possessed in memory.

The girl fingers her cloud of thick black hair, face expressing amazement at this newest fact. There was nothing like human hair on Homeworld.

His people have always been great. Much wiser than their conquerors. It was cooperation that brought peace to Homeworld, and cooperation they shall have again.

The human science books say his species lived 38 million years to humanity's own 2 million. Who knows if they are right? His people didn't measure time like humans do, and the humans seem only to remember only personal lives. They rely on artifacts and research to know their ancestors.

Jackson shudders. He cannot imagine being so deprived.

The First Ancestor's memories are his—millions or billions of years ago, the first mutant who passed on a memory of fear. From there, snatches of evolutionary history, the lineage of his ancestry stretching far, far to when his kind looked and thought differently. To when they fought each other.

Then came the World-Minds. The curators. It was they who brought peace and the way of wholeness. They who chose which memories to give him when they released his mother's egg into the sea.

They gave him memories of them. Of *being* them. World-Minds, the massive brains whose infinite knowledge made each moment ever-new. He remembers, dimly, flashes of insight like prophecy and thoughts like electrical storms. As much of them as his tiny brain can perceive, he remembers.

He fights again not to remember too much, not to fall into the human trap of grief. Grief would kill him. His ancestors knew that, so they gave him the ability to turn it off. It was a fine line they'd had to toe in his design; *remember, but do not despair.*

His people were greater than the humans in all aspects—except that crucial discovery, fire. That simple gift of brute force, natural to a species who evolved on hostile land outside the ocean's womb, had brought the humans across the stars and burned his people.

His people had mastered the powers of memory and time, of water and life. But the humans had the power of the sun, and the weakness of blind fear that still drove them to fight and kill.

Was that a weakness, or was it a strength? The humans had lost for themselves the opportunity to learn from his people, things that would have made them more than they imagined possible. But they'd won the battle for Homeworld; and his people, slow to strike, had lost.

Someday, this child and his others will sow children of their own. Someday, his people will be numerous again. Their children will have the gifts of fire and water, of sea and sky. There will be new World-Minds, and they will cross the stars.

For now, survival is slow and never certain.

But he has time. He has nothing, if not time.

Jackson holds his daughter's hand as they venture into the sunlight. The scarlet inferno of Agni is high in the west, the land that stretches before them is barren. Bharatha's infant life has not yet ventured from the sea that gave it birth.

He wonders if it will survive human predation long enough to do so. The quarantine zone the ecologists enforce already leaks like a sieve, more vicious Earth microbes devouring Bharatha's infant offspring.

Jackson fixes the child's helmet back onto her suit, triggering the vacuum seal. Reminds her not to break quarantine again in human sight, not to break any of the rules he imprinted in the human brain within her skull.

In time, her own neural tissue will overgrow the skull, replace the brain, and find niches in her bones. For now, the memories surviving in the human brain will keep her alive.

Overhead, a 'thopter wheels in the jade green sky. A rescue party, come to take them back to Bharatha's domed cities. Ecstatic, no doubt, at having found the missing child alive.

Jackson waves his arms to hail them.

THE DRAKE EQUATION

"The Drake Equation" was selected as a winner of the Writers of the Future Contest in 2016. It first appeared in print in *Writers of the Future Vol. 33.*

CAROL CLOSES HER EYES. Or tries to. Nothing changes. What she sees—a beach near her childhood home on Long Island—is the same whether her eyes are open or shut.

That's not good.

The pounding waves are a relaxing, rhythmic white noise. The distant traffic is another kind of white noise, more constant, the sound of haste. The white paint of the house behind her is chipped and cracked, weathered hard by the sea breeze. The sand is coarse gravel beneath her bare feet.

She hasn't been here since Ron—

—died.

Am I dead? Panic threatens.

Her rational mind thinks that highly unlikely. She has not believed in any sort of afterlife in years.

Yet here she is. And she can't explain how. She has never hallucinated. Never dreamt half so vividly. Never been so sure of being awake in an impossible place.

Oxygen deprivation could do this, maybe. She thinks back, strains to think back to before—

The hull was breached by a meteor. No pinprick—something the size of an all-terrain rover tore the ship clean in two at the passage connecting the command quarters to the hub. Too fast for the sensors to pick up, too fast to do anything even if they had seen it. This she deduced in the split-second before she was sucked out, the vacuum demanding her, her oxygen, and her books with equal ferocity.

For less than half a second as her eyes froze solid, she had seen the rest of the *Agena,* its pale sunlit form so deceptively small when viewed from the outside.

So near and yet so far.

No one will be able to reach me in time. That was certain.

Then *something* happened. Death or sleep or oxygen deprivation—

—and now she is here, standing barefoot on an achingly familiar Long Island beach.

And she can't close her eyes.

She is not alone.

The figure stands a few meters from her, his ankles lapped by cold surf. He is beautiful. His facial symmetry is heart-stopping, his features perfect.

Carol is very confused.

She'd never spent much time visualizing her ideal man, but apparently someone else has done it for her. And the presence of a stranger in what could otherwise have passed for a memory—concerns her.

Carol's heart skips a beat and her stomach flutters, and she pauses to wonder how that is possible if her body is freezing in space.

Wish fulfillment, she thinks. She has heard that the dying brain gives gifts—near-death experiences, rushes of endorphins, and the like. Hers is apparently her childhood home, and a handsome stranger. She half-expects her brother to come sauntering around the side of the house, as though he'd never left.

Her heart warms at the thought of that reunion. She smiles, glancing back towards the house.

To a good death.

But it is the stranger's voice that attracts her attention. "I'm sorry," he says, "if I startled you." His voice is soft and deep, gentle and powerful.

Blushing isn't something a dead person is supposed to be able to do, yet she is blushing.

And suspicious, both at once.

"And we are sorry," the stranger continues, "about—the interruption."

There is something off about his speech. Her own language center going? No—if that were it, his speech would sound normal to her. There is a problem with the meter of his speech, something deeply unsettling coming from so perfect a form.

Who's to say how hallucinations should behave?

And yet, something is wrong. Something more than what she'd thought.

She tries to speak to the stranger. Chokes. Like a schoolgirl approaching a crush. Blushes more furiously, this time in embarrassment which threatens to turn into anger.

The stranger smiles wryly.

"I apologize," he says again, a little wrongly, "for any distress. We were not sure—"

He flickers then, and all of reality flickers like old fluorescent lights. For fractions of a second, there seems to be *nothing*.

"—how best to approach you."

Carol barely heard him.

"Who are you?"

A broader smile. "We are—'aliens' is an alarming term, I'm told, in the lexicon of your people. But you don't seem to associate particular alarm with it."

It was true that "alarm" was not exactly the right word for the sensation that her stomach had dropped out of her body and was plummeting towards the Earth's core.

Hallucinating, she reminded herself desperately.

Although this is not entirely outside of the realm of wish fulfillment.

"We live somewhere—not physical," he says. "Somewhere else."

'Where else' can be parsed out later, if she still has a brain to parse with. But right now that seems academic, and a more burning question is:

"What's happening? Why me?"

He looks at her carefully, as though considering his words. "We apologize for—specimen collection."

"*Specimen collection?*" She had thought herself beyond indignation, but there it is. It combines with embarrassment to become anger. *This* doesn't seem to fit the wish fulfillment script.

"You blew me out into space for *specimen collection?*"

Nothing so cruel, she tells herself. *An act of random nature, not of will. This is a hallucination. My last dream.*

And yet—

And yet she had known, even as she felt the world sucked out from under her, that the odds of colliding with an object that size in near-Mars orbit were astronomically low. Had thought briefly that she might just be the first person in human history to be killed by a near-direct collision with a meteor.

The man whose face *still* sends her heart fluttering when she meets his eyes says: ""You will be—well cared-for. Your crew—is safe."

Suddenly, Carol feels very tired. If he is an alien—

"Can we drop the illusions, please?" she asks wearily.

The man smiles. "Not possible. Your mind will require time to adjust."

"I don't have eyes anymore, do I?"

"No," he confirmed gently.

"Will I ever have eyes again?"

"That remains to be seen."

<hr>

She sees nebulae. Nebulae as humans see them through false-color images, nebulae as they exist in the human lexicon, sprawling and beautiful and vast. That each dot within the glowing gas clouds is a sun, most of them with orbiting planets, is well beyond her ability to comprehend.

Humans think of nebulae as the nurseries of stars, but they are also graveyards.

The scientists back on Earth had said that the Population II stars could not have supported life. Said they were too poor in metals, in carbon, in every element beyond the hydrogen and helium birthed in the Big Bang. That the necessary materials for complex life—carbon at least, better with nitrogen and oxygen and other even heavier things—were lacking.

As the Population II stars lived, they created those building blocks of life through fusion in their cores. When they exploded in blinding glory, those building blocks were flung across parsecs to seed new star systems.

Humans thought of this as birth.

Her guide had introduced himself as "Daniel," and walked with her on the beach, the two of them alone, until he deemed her ready for something more.

Now he tells her how the birth of the nebulae had been death for his people.

We are an old form of life. Very old. Wise, we like to think. And yet still powerless.

You managed to ram a meteor into my ship, she reminds him, *and telepathically lifted me from my dying body. That seems pretty powerful to me.*

Power, he tells her, *is a relative term.*

He shows her the spread of his civilization.

It's like a dream.

He shows her not one civilization, but thousands; life and intellect and society spawning on a thousand worlds. From electrical impulses in the perpetual storms of gas giants, from chains of simple hydrocarbons in the roiling seas of massive gas giants, from crystals of ice in everlasting convection currents. In all of these places, she sees patterns form, change, re-form.

Wherever patterns form and change, the potential for self-replication exists.

Wherever self-replication began on those ancient worlds, so too did evolution.

"It still begins." Daniel corrects her, casting her eyes to a dozen, then a hundred watery, rocky worlds that no human scientist has ever heard of.

She is momentarily awed by this—then realizes something even stranger.

"When the stars you showed me died—that was billions of years ago. You are from—one of them?"

"Yes," Daniel confirms. *"We were lucky. We were taken."*

"Taken?"

"Lifted. Preserved. By another. Much as I took you. My people were naturally doomed. Old even then, far older than your race is now. We had survived long enough to overcome war. Not long enough to escape our dying Sun. That was—a mistake, on our parts.

He shows her something else, a layout of the galaxy and through it, a web of light, spreading.

"Only one species, he explains, *"had to learn the higher geometries well enough to live there. To draw on vacuum to perpetuate patterns of thought. Only one to teach the others. They took us before the end came."*

And she saw 'the end,' an explosion of light and heat and searing ultraviolet, of vital elements sowing the seeds of a dozen new stars with planets.

Planets like her own. Born from the deaths, not just of stars, but of civilizations. Parents they might never know.

If this was true, Daniel was more than five billion years old.

If he had been paying attention, he could have watched the Earth itself congeal from dust, seen the Moon thrown off in a titanic clash of worlds, watched the oceans condense out of a haze of water vapor and the first cells arise from the complex organic soup.

He would see Carol as a product of those cells—and human evolution as an infinitesimally tiny fraction of his own lifespan.

He would be, for all intents and purposes, a god.

Had he watched her species grow? Or had he been occupied elsewhere, part of some inconceivable, eternal society?

Carol is too afraid to ask.

"So," she no longer knows if she is dreaming, and no longer cares, *"both of my hypotheses were right."*

Daniel sends her waiting-silence.

"You're an alien. And this is also Heaven. The afterlife."

She doesn't like the tone of the silence he sends back.

"I mean, you take dying humans, don't you? You must. Why not? When do I get to see Ron?"

Silence.

"Answer me!"

"Please give us time," Daniel beseeches her, *"to explain it to you properly."*

There is a waiting that is much like death or sleep. And then there is a room, with people—aliens that look like things out of fantasy and science fiction sitting along its wall. Most of them are humanoid, and Carol is sure that this is for her benefit. She is standing in the middle as though on trial.

And she is angry.

"I am not an animal," she says, upon flickering back into consciousness. "Don't tranquilize me just because you don't want to deal with me."

Daniel sits at the head of the council, and it is he who says: "We apologize. Your pattern made it clear that you would not accept distractions. You asked the right questions more quickly than we expected. We needed to prepare."

"Prepare *what*?"

Carol feels oddly betrayed by his words. By his very presence standing *with* the others and *against* her. His disguise worked well enough that she'd stopped thinking of it as a disguise. Started thinking of him as a friend.

Not human. She finds her mind is quick to jump to that now that she feels offended.

She feels offended with good reason. *They are the ones who killed me. They are the ones who do not care about people like me.*

But something nags at her. Some part of her has not yet managed to shake her belief, perhaps because of his beauty, in Daniel's inherent *goodness*.

The council is silent. Not answering her question. Glancing at each other, murmuring to each other in words she cannot understand. She feels as though this is some sort of answer.

We had to prepare this council to judge you.

"You're damn right I won't accept distractions!" she fumes. Remembers losing faith in the God of her childhood, in all gods.

Remembers why. The image of the judge sitting on the throne, ready to condemn, indifferent to his own responsibility.

"You have great power. You have a *duty*. You can do for others what they cannot do for themselves. If you can bring me here, if there is no technical limitation—*you should be saving everyone who dies*. Regardless of species. Regardless of merit. Answer the question I asked before: do you save the people who die on Earth? Do you let them walk among you?"

She is confronted with hope, the greatest hope humanity has ever had; and with it, the threat of losing her faith all over again.

A long silence gives her answer.

A glowing woman with fairy wings stirs uncomfortably to Daniel's left, avoids Carol's gaze. Seems a mockery of the magical creature she resembles, until the tears begin to pour down her fluorescent cheeks.

"No," Daniel says.

Carol is confused again. Why is the immortal woman crying? Why does Daniel seem sad, genuinely sad—

Sudden hope flares again.

"*Can* you save them?" she asks swiftly. "Is there some sort of technical problem? Is that why you're studying me? Please, study away—"

"No," Daniel cuts her off. "We could save them. It is not beyond our capabilities."

She stares at him, at a loss.

"You," he says, "are an astronaut."

She doesn't see what that has to do with anything.

"Tested for your ability to work in teams. In close quarters. To resolve conflicts. To put mission before yourself."

"Yes."

"And you are—an astrosociologist." Daniel tilted his maddeningly, heartbreakingly, rage-inducingly beautiful head at her. "Your chosen path is to think about people like us."

"Yes."

She finds that she does not care, now, whether she has truly realized her life's goal. The question of whether she stands before true alien intelligence or the hallucination of a dying mind rings hollow. She looks to the weeping fairy, who meets her eyes with wells of great liquid sadness.

She remembers the sight of the *Agena* slipping away from her, so near, so hopelessly out of reach. Remembers the oxygen rushing from her lungs and into the hungry void.

Remembers her brother dying back on Earth at the tender age of thirty-four, his liver too badly riddled with cancer to filter the toxins from his blood. The cancer had also infiltrated half a dozen organs, but it was the liver failure that killed him.

She raises her eyes to Daniel's again, looking for an answer. "Why?"

"You know about the Drake Equation."

Yes. She does. The equation for calculating the total number of extraterrestrial civilizations in the galaxy. It has no known solution, because the value of so many of its component parts are unknown.

In the past century, humans had gained insight into two of the variables: the rate of star formation and the average number of planets per star. Both numbers turned out to be vast. There were trillions of planets, in all likelihood, in the Milky Way alone.

But other essentials were still unknown. The number of planets capable of supporting life; the number of life-bearing planets which become civilized—and Carol's area of expertise, of study and questioning:

How long do civilizations survive after they develop technology?

The troubling thing, of course, was that until now, the answer to the Drake Equation was "one." Only one civilization in the Milky Way galaxy was known to humans—their own. No other radio signals had ever reached the lonely ears in the desert, the massive radio telescope arrays built to seek companionship out there in the infinite void.

That meant that one of the unknown variables—the probability of life, the likelihood of civilization, or the lifespan of a civilization once it developed sufficient technology to broadcast radio waves—had to be so vanishingly small as to reduce a trillion planets to just a single civilization existing in this space and time.

It would have been Carol's wish, would have been the best thing her dying brain could give her, to believe she had found a myriad of other civilizations. That the infinite Universe was not entirely hostile to life, that it might have been designed for it in some way. That civilization was not a flickering anomaly, vanishingly rare or comically short-lived.

Is this real? It can't be.

She studies the aliens in the chamber around her. She no longer has eyes, and these people, if they exist at all, no longer have bodies. Are they choosing their own appearances, or is it her own mind which crafts the woman with the shining fairy wings at Daniel's right and the ponderously long-necked creature at his left?

"What," she asks quietly "does the Drake Equation have to do with anything?"

"You are interested in the lifespan of a civilization."

"Yes."

"Do you know what determines that?"

Carol smiles bitterly. If she did, how many Nobel prizes would she have?

"Violence," Daniel says simply. "Violence is good for non-technological species. It helps them live long enough to become what they are. But technological development, once it has taken off—must not be paired with violence. The lifespan of civilizations that retain violence in their technological age is vanishingly short."

Carol is still waiting to hear what this has to do with her question.

"Your species is violent. How can we risk introducing them to the level of technology we possess?"

What he is suggesting seems laughable.

"You're saying we'd destroy you?"

"You might. We might not be able to stop you. To free your minds would be to open the gates of hell for a thousand species that came before you. We collect specimens—rarely— to see if you have yet outgrown this malady."

"So you chose me," she says steadily, "because I have studied human history."

"Yes."

"Do you want me to judge them for you?"

"No. We wanted to study your reactions."

The truth that's settling into her bones could well be insanity-inducing.

Her people don't have to die. Ever.

People like her brother don't have to die—if she can convince these people that they can be trusted with godlike power.

And she can't.

She cannot even try. Not in good conscience.

The hatred and sense betrayal that roils in her own heart at Daniel's actions, at his revelations, bear testament to that.

She cannot even tell them that *she* can be trusted with power. Not now. Not knowing what they have refused to do in order to preserve themselves. How soon would she grow angry enough to learn how to kill these immortals?

What about Ron? What would it have taken to turn him to deadly force?

Not enough. Not enough to risk it.

She suspects that they can see this. That in her eyes, humanity has already failed a crucial test. How long until they test again? A century? More? A hundred years would be the blink of an eye to these people.

Daniel's mind wraps around her, gentle, warm, nurturing. *You've done the right thing*, he tells her. *You have been honest.*

And she sees through his mind, as he sees through hers—that her honesty, her failure to insist violently that his people save hers, is itself a sign of progress.

A small comfort. Not enough for a woman who has seen what might have been, what may yet be, what is.

What will they do with me now?

She doesn't know; it doesn't matter.

And what about her people? That species struggling to life around an infant star?

In a millennium or three, we may be ready.

SKY CHILDREN

I wrestled with whether to include "Skychildren" in this collection. With the Own Voices movement requesting that people stick to writing their own ethnic groups, I now try to avoid writing viewpoint characters whose heritage I do not share. I have updated some details of this story in hopes of mitigating these concerns. But changing Chinwe's race always felt wrong. And excluding her felt worse.

"Skychildren" was first published in Issue 5 of *Compelling Science Fiction* in March of 2019. It appeared again in print in "Compelling Science Fiction: The First Collection." It has been translated into Vietnamese by Long Nguyễn for the Vietnamese fanzine SFVN.

Chinwe has become a monster.

She had known that it would be part of the assignment. They warned her about what she'd have to do to fit in. She had signed the forms, but none of it had seemed real until the first time her teacher had approached her with a needle.

On this boat she'd be the odd one out if she *didn't* look like an alien.

The residents of the *Orún* are all adapted to make some of their own nutrients and oxygen from the light of the fusion core. The *Orún's* children still need to eat and breathe, but the engineers cheerfully remind Chinwe that all progress comes from experimentation each time she visits them for a new injection. In time, they hoped to eliminate those needs.

Bright growing lights are everywhere here; warm white by day, dimmed to a pink that incorporates only the wavelengths most nourishing to chloroplasts by night. Gigawatts more power pour from *Orún's* core into batteries: for the shuttles, for the outposts, for *Orún's* own emergency backup systems (though with fusion at its heart, the asteroid is more likely to overheat than experience a power outage).

The vast majority of core's power is creatively wasted; through temperature regulators, convection pumps, and any other mechanism anyone could come up with to do the job.

The hardest job on *Orún* is staying cool. Core overload is the nightmare no one speaks of. It's an appropriate metaphor: a community threatened by the excess of its own power and ambition. This is not a place for the cautious. *Orún* is for those willing to give all to craft a new future.

It isn't easy to hide a small star in space. Even among Belt colonies, *Orún* is huge. And as far as the law is concerned, it isn't supposed to exist.

That's why Chinwe is here.

She bares her teeth at her reflection in the silvered polymer mirror of her bathroom. The "bathroom" is open to the artificial breezes of the residential shell, like every structure on this level. The shell's surface area of several kilometers combines with the random number generator that runs the ventilation system to make it feel almost like the open air of Earth.

Almost. Chinwe still aches for the original, with its blue sky and fluffy clouds, an unimaginable amount of unused air and water. Yet she has adjusted quickly, the familiarity of Earth flooded out by the riot of intense newness that is *Orún*.

Has it been weeks since her arrival, not decades?

Here they have breezes, at least, and there is grass sprouting from the cracks strategically designed to look random in the floor and walls.

Her reflection is as green as the grass, but darker—a dense onyx-emerald. The engineers offered to inhibit her melanin production so that her chloroplasts would get more light, but Chinwe declined. And they had understood. Blackness was one of the few traits they respected.

Even her teeth are black, now—carbon steel implants which she grudgingly admits she doesn't mind. They will never rot. When she first saw the photographs of people with these teeth, she had thought they looked awful—like cosmetics done in terrible taste. But now she appreciates the fact that, were she back home, she could take out an armed suspect with them.

Chinwe pauses, flexes a black-green arm under the bright glowing lights. She isn't bulletproof. Not yet. The Skychildren are still working on that.

And she is still working on stopping them.

Walking in the centrifugal gravity is easy for her, now.

For the first few weeks she'd been like a newborn calf. The slight difference in centrifugal force between her head and her feet had made her sick when she wasn't on a constant anti-nausea regimen, and sent her careening into countless walls and pieces of furniture even when she was. But by now, she has adapted.

So have the four of her compatriots who survived the first round of injections.

Not "compatriots." Not "friends." Chinwe chides herself. She was trained exhaustively to look, act, speak like one of them —but she is not one of them. None of them know who she truly is. They accept her as one of their own. Accept that she, like them, seeks meaning.

Chinwe must admit that this place has its charms. There are no drug dealers, no loan sharks, and no need for either; there is no money, full employment, no outsiders. Everyone has a place. If a resident of *Orún* does not fit into an existing niche, one is created for them. No talent or predisposition is wasted.

Four of the youth who accompanied her are alive and happy here. The fifth died screaming, arteries slashed open by his own carbon steel claws.

There is a price for everything.

A price for paradise. A price to drift in the space between worlds, powered by your own private sun. A price to please the necessary investors to finance such a massive illegal operation. To impress the rich folks who also get to feel part of something, who get to believe that they too are shaping humanity's destiny of freedom from the restrictions of the habitable worlds.

Adele "Mama" Nwosu is very good at attracting investors. Chinwe still remembers the PR vid that her recruit showed her in the basement of a tattoo parlor. A slender green girl with a cloud of hair about her head, leaping to pluck fruit from an intensely bioengineered tree. The five teenagers in her "class" had been attracted by the same vid. Attracted to invest their lives in creating a new world.

The sisters had come from a town in the northwest.

Afraid of strangers, they'd clung to each other like shadows. The brothers had come from a local slum, two already with extensive histories of survival crimes and the third in danger of the same. His brothers had sought out the Skychildren more for his sake than for their own.

The one who had clawed his arteries open had been the oldest, charged with murder back on Earth after throwing someone down a flight of stairs. He'd pled self-defense, but had served time anyway. His brothers were told that it was suicide, that the "empathy genes" they'd been testing were to blame.

Chinwe doesn't know how she feels about empathy genes. Her teacher has explained to her the genetic variance in oxytocin receptors, which affect the mirror neurons that allow a person to feel another's experiences as though they were their own. Her teacher has shown her all the data about the strength of the correlation between this gene variant and pro-social, compassionate behavior. Lots of hard data, lots of hard facts.

But she finds she doesn't believe it. The human mind is a funny thing.

Her teacher is coming now—Ariel is emerald green and naked in the warm pumped air but for strings of ornamental beads around her waist and neck. Residents of *Orún* lose their love for clothing over time, surrounded by the constant heat and no judgement except for that of wasted effort.

Ariel says that it has been four years for her, since she jumped ship on Earth in a bout of teenage angst. She doesn't regret it. Chinwe wonders what happens to people who do regret it, after they have learned too much.

She tries not to think about that. She now knows too much.

Like all the residents of *Orún* except for Mama Nwosu's handpicked cadre of experts, Ariel is younger than Chinwe.

In adults, the promotional materials explain, stem cells and tissues lose their flexibility. Chinwe was picked for this assignment in part because she's been mistaken for a pre-teen all her life. In reality she's twenty-seven, an enforcer with five years' experience under her belt.

Ariel walks with a spring in her step. Chinwe finds that she does now, too. It might be the lower gravity. It might be a cult member's pathology of joy, of having found something *better* than the outside world.

Memories of poor dead Akeem do alarmingly little to stop the flow of Chinwe's thoughts about this place. What would Ariel be doing back on Earth? High school, perhaps? Whining at her parents about the woes of a privileged life, as Bridget Van Aalst had done before her disappearance? Isn't this, in a real way, better?

Stop that. Chinwe cringes at herself. A twenty percent risk of death before the age of twenty is not "better" than anything.

Chinwe smiles a little too easily, baring teeth at Ariel as she approaches. "New recruits?" she asks, slowing her pace to meet the other.

Ariel shakes her head, grins showing glinting carbon-fiber in return. "Going to the core. Teachers' retreat with the Adaptives starts today."

Chinwe nods, curiosity suddenly burning like a fusion fire in her belly. The 'Adaptives' are one of four branches of something like clergy. Their full-time employment is to meditate on the founding principles of *Orún*, with the authority to restructure its operations as they see fit. It is not unheard of for an Adaptive or an Intentional or some other overseer to arrive at a laboratory or residence and entirely rearrange things. This core of thinkers is allowed to contro-vert any rule or routine they see fit, thus saving *Orún* from the risks of dogma and stasis.

The Adaptives are revered almost as angelic beings, venerated second only to Nwosu herself. Chinwe has never spoken with one, never seen them except for the occasional speeches and flashes of brightly colored fabric at a distance.

And soon these people might be gone forever from their natural habitat.

"Can I come with you?" she asks Ariel, her own words surprising her.

Ariel looks at Chinwe, seeming much wiser than her nineteen years. Slowly, she nods. "The retreat is meant for teachers. But perhaps that is the path you're meant for."

"I have flex time this week," Chinwe assures her.

Ariel reaches for her hand. Holding hands—that's another inhibition one loses on *Orún*.

As they walk beneath lab-created lianas, passing the grass-sprouting mounds of private quarters, Chinwe remembers the end of her life on Earth.

'A once in a lifetime opportunity,' her commissioner had told her from across the metal table of the briefing room.

'You could help take down one of the largest human trafficking rings in the world. The risk would be great.' The commissioner knew that Chinwe had never shied from risks.

At some level, Chinwe knew what this was. The docket she'd been handed had listed the rich girls who disappeared, whose parents quietly made gifts to the Department out of their own pockets. It did not list not the countless hundreds who quietly went missing from the slums. But anything that would stop the people who were taking both was the right thing to do. Wasn't it?

She had never yet regretted her decision. Questioned it, yes. But never regretted it. Especially not after listening to an informant weep as he recounted the death of a girl he'd loved like a daughter.

'They didn't mean to kill her,' he'd said. *'But she wanted out. Sometimes the memory blocks they use do that. They know it. Eighty-percent survival rate, they say. Eighty percent if you defect. Eighty percent if you stay. It's not enough. It's not enough.'*

That had closed Chinwe's decision. Officially, she was assigned to recover Bridget Van Aalst and the children of other privileged families. But the Skychildren took far more children of the poor than of the rich—and killed far more, by extension.

Walking beneath the lianas, Chinwe shudders. The image of the Adaptives she is going to see, of the green woman holding her hand, twist in her mind. One moment Ariel is a teacher, preternaturally wise; the next she is a child who has been deceived into slavery. One moment the Adaptives are angelic beings, more conscious of true reality than any earthly clergy; the next they are twisted children who only think that they serve God.

The Adaptives' color is red. The red of fire and blood, her Needs teachers have told her. The red of danger and of vital life; the red of animals, hunters and hunted, subject to natural selection.

That is why the Adaptives wear red sashes. It's a stark and jarring contrast to the blues, greens, and whites that are ubiquitous throughout *Orún.*

Anything on the asteroid that can be alive and green is, on the inner levels—everywhere green and white, growing lights and grass and hanging lianas. And the outermost shell is blue—a sea in space, combination water tank, aquaculture, and radiation shield. The *Orún* sea is lit from above and below by growing lights, and thick with kelp and other sea life, and all residents visit for at least a few days each month to assist with the harvest. These are the places Chinwe has known in the weeks since her arrival.

Being ushered into the Adaptive's inner sanctum is almost a physical shock. *Everything* is red here.

Ruby-bright LEDs lace every inch of the ceiling in elaborate patterns. The adaptives' sashes, red in daylight, appear white here as they reflect all available wavelengths—all red. The green skin of the supplicants appears uniformly jet black, *absorbing* all available light. Chinwe observes with fascination that her skin and Ariel's turn the same color, here.

The air is *warm*—warmer even than *Orún* normal, warm like the heat of Nigeria at noon, warm like the train compartment on the ride she took through its great national forests. She wonders if the warmth is intentional, or unavoidable—because the inner sanctum of the clergy is on the level closest to the fusion reactor, *Orún*'s true Holiest of Holies.

This is both symbolic and pragmatic, her Needs curriculum explains. The Adaptives, Intentionals, Creatives, and Living represent the highest form of human thought, that which can be devoted purely to imagination, data analysis, invention, and celebration of life. As such, they fly closest to the Sun.

However, the functions of the Adaptives and their kin are also the least necessary to the short-term survival of a society. If *Orún*'s reactor blows, it is the Exalted Ones who will go first, who will have the least chance to escape. The common laborers, the harvesters, will have the greatest chance to survive, for they have the best chance of rebuilding their society.

As a side effect of their proximity to the core—and

perhaps also as an intentional choice—there is almost no gravity in the Adaptives' inner sanctum. Chinwe feels as though she might blow away in any passing breeze, finds herself straining, uncomfortably, to keep her feet on the ground.

Toes and soles barely touch the floor. It's so easy to accidentally push off and take ten or twenty seconds to drift back down. The Adaptive's red/white sashes billow angelically in the slight air currents. Their wearers seem to simply fly as they spring and perch from the floor to a network of thin wires, invisible in the dim light.

Before coming to *Orún* such a hot, red space would have carried associations with Hell. Now it's just so disorientingly *different* that the connotations of divinity are easy to see. *Orún* has taught her to associate the different, not the comfortable, with the divine.

An Adaptive drops down to meet the tour group consisting of Chinwe, Ariel, and a dozen other students. Chinwe barely manages to stay silent as the shock of recognition rattles through her body.

The Adaptive is Bridget Van Aalst. The missing girl from the pictures.

Chinwe didn't recognize the young woman while she was up on the wires. But now the sharp nose and cheekbones are unmistakable. And the mischievous grin. The hint of rebelliousness at the corners of the mouth.

Van Aalst had vanished from her father's mansion along with $600,000 drained from his bank account five years earlier. She'd been described as a "troubled" seventeen year-old with several known substance addictions who had once been sent to a boot camp in the wilderness after wiring large amounts of her father's money to an online boyfriend.

Upon her return, things had seemed normal for a few months—but then she'd disappeared. An exhaustive inventory of her electronic communications had revealed conversations with a faceless screenname called "Adam"—the same screenname she'd wired the money to a year earlier.

The Adam screenname had been untraceable, bouncing off of multiple satellites before reaching Van Aalst's terminal —and all leads in the case of her disappearance had gone cold until a man from Nigeria contacted the FBI four years later, claiming to have helped arrange her illegal passage into orbit out of a Texas spaceport.

'*Look at me now, Daddy,*' Chinwe thinks as Van Aalst descends angelic to the floor. Her hair billows about her head, lit up like a halo in the red light, and her sashes glow dazzling scarlet-white against the darkness of her skin.

Van Aalst seems to look directly at Chinwe as she smiles, and Chinwe can do nothing about the sense of growing panic clawing at her gut.

There is no way Van Aalst can know that Chinwe is looking for her. Just because Chinwe stared at her picture throughout her last months on Earth, until she felt she knew the troubled teen intimately, does not mean that Van Aalst has any way to recognize *her.*

Yet Van Aalst's appearance has changed the very air in the room. This is no longer a pleasant dream. It is something like a nightmare.

She hopes her sweat can be explained away by the heat, that her staring can be explained as awe.

"I am—Chinwe. Six weeks' new. A student."

By the time they get to her in the introductions, Chinwe's body has gone into crisis mode. Her years of experience in appearing fierce is returning. This is just like a combat situation.

Except that she's roughly one hundred million miles from Earth, alone in an asteroid full of cultists, and her nearest backup is four days away at top speed. She can't even hail them unless she can get back to the upload port in her quarters.

Still. Her adrenaline levels have stabilized now, and this is beginning to become fun.

Everyone else in the tour group turns out to be of teacher rank—Chinwe, a student not yet out of her first semester at *Orún*, must explain herself.

"I—met Ariel on her way here, today. Asked where she was going. I had flex time, wanted to come, so I came."

Chinwe lowers her face, unable to meet Van Aalst's sharp-toothed smile, as much to stay in character as because of genuine discomfort.

"We don't normally take first semester students," the Adaptive chastises gently. "This is a place for deep thought. You barely have the underpinnings."

"I studied in the States," Chinwe blurts. "Biology. Early admit to college. Accelerated program."

This is true enough—she'd considered medical school before realizing that she hated formal education and opting for the academy instead. The "early admit" and "accelerated" parts are lies, but the only way to explain her first admission without blowing her cover.

"Ahh." Van Aalst sits back, pleasure and surprise painting her features. "That is something. Not many of us here brought that level of education from Earth. You will learn at least as much in your courses here, and more organically. But what an interesting perspective. What did they teach you, Chinwe, about evolution?"

"That it functions through natural selection," she recites, verbatim, from her Basic Needs of Organisms class—*Orún*-based, but similar enough to what she learned at Emory. "Or, at least, it did—before the advent of genetic engineering." Chinwe pauses, looking to Van Aalst to see her verdict.

"Oh, it still functions through natural selection," Van Aalst agrees. "But now we can give it help. Dumb organisms must rely on mutation to create new traits at random. Most of them are harmful. We—we can design our own new traits. Consciously."

Chinwe nods dutifully.

Beneath the exterior of rapt student, her two personas are wrestling—the fictional Chinwe-Niece-of-Javier still awed by Van Aalst's poise and title, Chinwe-L.A.P.D. poised to go on the offensive.

"What did they teach you about genetic modification," Van Aalst asks, "at your university on Earth?"

Chinwe glances around at the other adaptives hanging like angels in the rafters, carrying on secret conversations with each other in hushed tones.

"They taught that it was—dangerous. Certain cosmetic therapies are common among the wealthy now, and gene therapy to cure diseases is very common. Genetic modification of crops is good. But new treatments for humans take a long time to be approved. They have to be deemed very safe. Or bad things can happen."

"What sorts of bad things?"

"Deaths. Three of them, in the past century. Runaway immune responses. Deemed unacceptable. Research must not introduce risk to those who are not already in danger."

Van Aalst nods sagely, and Chinwe can feel her cheeks burning. This earthly attitude is directly contradictory to the trailblazing attitude of *Orún*, and under the pressure of Van Aalst's gaze Chinwe feels almost ashamed to support the former.

"How long," Van Aalst asks, "to get a new treatment to market, on Earth?"

Chinwe dredges that information up, from a memory of another world.

"Five years. Average. Three or four rounds of clinical trials with small groups. Exhaustive analysis to confirm no added risk. One vaccine—they said it prevented thousands from contracting illness, but sixteen people had neurological side effects so its approval was revoked."

Van Aalst pushes off the ground slightly, seeming at once to become playful and to gain imposing height.

"So," she says, "on Earth, they introduce new and beneficial mutations at a snail's pace. And—here's the key—*only reactively*. They make the body work the way it's supposed to. The way it used to. Not the way it *could*, if they scrapped the old design and their old assumptions."

Van Aalst reaches up, seizes an invisible wire above her head, and pirouettes around it in a backflip. Red-white sashes billow and expose her bare, dark body below the waist before she launches herself horizontally and sails across half the chamber.

"Fly with me!" she commands.

The hands-on lesson is instructive; you cannot soar in Earth gravity.

They are breaking for a meal in the Blue Room when the emissary comes for her.

The Blue Room—home of the Intentionals, who are pure, cold intellect to the Adaptives' exuberant fire—is darker than the Adaptives' home. The walls are black but for geometric illustrations in blazing blue. Chinwe recognizes a few of them—one is an illustration of the Golden Ratio, intersecting, she thinks, with an illustration of the paths of the planets around the Sun.

The meal is unusual, even for *Orún*. It's mostly protein refined from kelp and yeast—that's not unusual—but it's flavored and colored in bizarre ways. One of Chinwe's entrees is radiating its own blue light.

Her intellect knows that means it was fresh-harvested from a plant imbued with the genes of bioluminescent jellyfish, but her emotions refuse to see it as anything other than radioactive—or maybe heavenly.

A previously hidden door opens in a wall near the dining supplicants. "Chinwe Ondongo," a man asks, peering in, "would you please come with me?"

Her fear at having sighted Van Aalst has cooled by now, and she does not think this overly strange—*Orún's* workings are not well spelled-out in any way that a newcomer can understand, and with each newcomer on their own unique development path, it is not wholly unusual for individuals to be summoned elsewhere without warning. Perhaps it's her Needs teacher, or perhaps the kelp team is short today after all.

Chinwe rises and walks. She's half-nervous that she is in trouble for skipping her portion of today's aquaculture rotation—she normally loves kicking through the depths of the ocean-in-space, but today was an opportunity she couldn't pass up. And the teams usually have a bit of "flex" room which can be made up later in the week.

But soon her spine begins to tingle. The door that is held open for her seems to open onto nothing. Black space—a floor, clearly, because her escort is standing on it, but her eyes perceive only black. Police mode resurging, she makes note of his features the way you would a suspect's—mostly African, perhaps one European grandparent, dreadlocks, Caribbean origin by the way he walks and speaks.

He regards her with imperious grace, odd for *Orún* but less odd for the Intentionals' corner of it. He gestures her into the blackness impatiently, and she ignores her officers' instinct not to follow the strange man into the dark alley.

"Where are we going?" Chinwe asks with the obedient curiosity of a good student. Against her will, she glances back at the pool of blue light retreating behind the closing door.

"You do want to meet Nwosu, don't you?"

Suddenly there is ice in Chinwe's veins.

Meet Adele Nwosu? She's not sure if this is a supreme honor being offered to a precocious student, or a death sentence for a spy.

Images of Nwosu dance before Chinwe's eyes, mostly drawn from decades'-old holos made before the woman disappeared. She lives in Chinwe's mind as an elegant young woman in lavender silk—a visionary, a mystic, an entrepreneur—who disappeared amid allegations that she had charmed a series of rich men into supporting illegal human genetic experimentation.

Nwosu had been a dock worker in Lagos herself to start, the daughter of two farmers who moved to the slums to give her a better education. The education had taken, even if conventional success hadn't. Eventually she had met a businessman on a layover who had taken her to Belgrade to meet his investor friends.

Adele Nwosu had been a beautiful and charismatic thirty-something before her disappearance. She'd have to be middle-aged now.

And she was here. That alone filled in a huge blank in the LAPD's knowledge. Chinwe thinks of the cruiser force, four days out, coming to extract her and evacuate *Orún.*

"Adele Nwosu? Why?"

"Hell if I know," her escort responds eloquently. He is invisible now, ahead of her in the darkness. She feels her way with each step, fingers trailing along the wall to keep her going straight.

She realizes then that this is the deepest darkness she has seen since settling on *Orún* four months ago. It has to be intentional. Nothing grows here—no white or pink growing lights, no cracks for grass to sprout out of. The floor beneath her feet feels like polished stone.

Her guides' footsteps stop, and a door begins to open. She sees that he is standing aside to admit her.

A soft pink-orange radiance pours in. It is not like the pink lights of night, not like anything Chinwe has seen since leaving—

Earth.

The door opens onto a garden, lush with plants with huge emerald leaves, delicate spring-like vines, and dark, swollen berries swaying in the breeze. The lighting is the color of dawn, and Chinwe catches glimpses of pink and violet between the leaves.

By the gravity, they're still on the level of the inner sanctum—but this place clearly belongs to none of the four branches.

Only inches from her face, a brown hand pushes a curtain of leaves aside.

"Hello, Chinwe Contee. I have been watching you."

Contee. Her real name. American name, LAPD name, FBI name. Nwosu knows. How long has she known?

Nwosu's face has grown round with age, but she's a young fifty-something, and she is smiling as she emerges from behind a thick curtain of hanging lilies.

She is the only person Chinwe has seen since on *Orún* who isn't green.

Chinwe says nothing. There is nothing to say.

"You don't seem surprised to see me." Nwosu smiles, a crooked, mother's smile.

"I've gotten good at hiding my surprise."

Nwosu steps towards her, apparently unafraid. It strikes

Chinwe that this is absurd—Nwosu is nude and clearly unarmed, older, and has probably been living in microgravity for decades. Chinwe could win in a fight easily—could kill Nwosu with her bare hands if it came to it.

Of course, it won't come to it. This is Nwosu's turf, no way off for four days. Chinwe wonders how the Skychildren would handle someone who tried to kill their founder. She has never heard of an attempted homicide on *Orún*.

"What are you going to do with me?" Chinwe asks.

"I am going to let you choose."

Chinwe's eyebrows go up, and she's surprised to feel herself smiling. "You would place your people's fate in my hands?"

"No," Nwosu concedes. "Only your own."

It's death or allegiance, then. Allegiance: stay; or refuse, and die. She knows nobody gets off of *Orún*.

Does she dare to lie? Does she dare to tell the truth?

"The Belt Authority already knows where we are. They're en route. Four days away. Kill me and add murder to the list of crimes you will face."

Nwosu smiles, and Chinwe thinks suddenly of the girl who died in Javier's care. "I will already face charges of murder if I return to Earth."

Chinwe is silent at that. Considers springing, grappling her, trusting that Nwosu was too confident to have guards waiting in the thick foliage.

Adele taps her head and points at Chinwe. At Chinwe's skull, she realizes. At the chip in her brain that her falsified medical records said was a stimulator for a motor cortex fried by bad heroin.

"How long have you known?" Chinwe asks.

"Only a day. Our sensor fields caught the signal you sent out last night. I have been thinking very hard about what to do with you since breakfast."

Nwosu cannot possibly be offering her mercy.

That *Orún* still exists is a testament to Nwosu's thoroughness in expunging elements who might betray them. Chinwe has learned in the course of her months here that *Orún*'s agents interact with dozens of Belt mining stations on a regular basis.

She knows from her FBI briefing that her agents, when captured, have a nasty habit of committing suicide rather than revealing any information about the asteroid.

And she knows from her catechism with Nwosu's agents in Nigeria that no one is allowed to return to Earth after they have seen *Orún.*

"You cannot trust me," Chinwe says. "You know that."

Adele's eyes rest on her with a heavy curiosity. "Do I?"

Chinwe feels the hairs on her arms stand up. She feels it now, the force of personality that has convinced dozens of people to give their wealth and freedom to make this dream a reality.

A bastion of human experimentation, beyond the reach of earthbound law enforcement, to advance the human race.

That most procedures worked best on those not long past puberty was a mere nuisance, which Adele explained by saying that she believed in children's right to self-determination. The right to choose their own futures.

Chinwe wonders; the adaptive abilities of a child's body are well-documented, but aren't children also more vulnerable to indoctrination?

Chinwe hates this woman.

And loves what she has created.

Orún. To walk through the residences, to swim through the kelp. The Adaptives. The Intentionals. The fusion core between the stars.

"Why would you ever think that you could trust me?" she asks.

Nwosu is still studying her with unnerving intensity. "You chose to go to the Adaptives today. The day after you reported us, you broke your routine to go there. And we decoded your report; it's incomplete. You could have told them so much more."

Chinwe's face is burning.

"You did your duty. Followed the letter of your law—and then you went to the Adaptives. You probably told yourself that you had to see them before they were destroyed. But you never really wanted to destroy them, did you? You complied with your superiors' orders out of fear of them. You went to the Adaptives out of love."

"What do you know about love?" Chinwe spits at her, remembering Akeem, the boy who died screaming.

"Quite a lot, actually," Adele says softly. What other force do you think brought me here?"

Egomania. Messiah complex. Words from her briefings back on Earth buzz through her head. But what she finally says is: "Pride."

Adele's laugh is light and musical. She is moving toward Chinwe again. "Yes," she laughs. "Pride. Pride caused me to become a fugitive. To forfeit any right to return to the world of my birth."

"You do not love these people."

"Who are you trying to convince, Chinwe? Yourself, or me?"

Chinwe wants to realize that talking will do no good. She does not want uncertainty. She wants a death sentence. Wants the certainty of Mama's cruelty, wants to be gone when the agents arrive to tear this place apart—

She wants to at least *want* to go back to Los Angeles. She wants to be sad about the prospect that she may never return.

"I'm not going to give you what you think you deserve, Chinwe. I'm giving you a choice."

Chinwe waits.

"If you stay, the chip comes out. Right now. I have attendants waiting in the back with sedatives. The chip is removed, no harm, no foul. And you have no way to contact Earth. We move *Orún*. Four days gives us time to get far away from here. You can stay. Or you can die."

Chinwe feels like she is dying.

And she is not, she is *not* going to cry in front of Adele Nwosu.

Nwosu reaches for Chinwe. Chinwe lets Nwosu fold her in her arms.

———

Orún station glides away from the shade of the companion asteroid that has shielded it for so long. It is silent as nightfall, cloaked with fields and geometries poached from the secrets of the Earth's best militaries. Its mass is void-black, visible as nothing but a brief eclipsing of the stars.

SHEANNA

This is Sheanna's first publication, following a gaggle of "we *almost* bought her" letters from major spec fic magazines. She's a little bit old school, but I like her for that reason.

———

SHE REMEMBERS when the planets formed. The condensation of the atoms from primordial fire, the light of creation blooming into the darkness of the void. She remembers matter condensing, circling, falling inward until atoms fused, liberating the fires of creation stored within.

She remembers dust becoming—

This. A bird sings outside her window, its vocal cords a delicate mesh of atoms. The bird sings its lungs out, pumping molecules of air through a sharp tiny beak in an effort to attract a mate.

Mating. This is how animals propagate. But not gods.

It is strange to think that humans are animals like any others. She has taken their form for so long that she forgets how this shape originated. It is easy to think of them as godforms. So easy. Until one of them missteps.

The humans crave gods who look like them, even while reaching for something higher. They are not rational.

She finds she loves them anyway.

She loves especially the one named Marcus, who was once a child, who is now a young adult, who will flower through manhood and old age in what will seem a span of breaths to her. She's seen it before. She will miss him when he dies.

This bothers her. The Divine should not feel attachment to temporary forms.

She looks across her throne room—a small space, made for intimacy and carved out of solid stone. Windows in the outward-facing wall have no need for glass in the equatorial spring. The openings permit her worship space to breathe freely of the sun and air. These are, after all, her kin.

The little bird hops off of the window ledge, descends in a fluttering swoop to the rug-strewn floor. The rugs are woven of the finest wool, dyed in every color, each rug a gift from a worshipper, each telling a story through symbol. Some of them are supplications; others simply praise. Some were complicated magic, weaving together carefully chosen symbolic elements towards the weaver's goal. Others were artists' achievements of pure aesthetics. The two have much in common.

The little bird hops around on one of them, a spell-rug of gold, magenta, and scarlet that had been woven by a farmer hoping for a bountiful crop to bring him luck in love. Sheanna had made it happen, and he had grown old and died a happy man with many children. His rug lives on, a testament to his ambition.

Children are another thing that she will never understand. Divinities are born old; they do not need to be reared into it. What must it be like, she wonders, to have a growing brain?

Soon, her attendants will be out to beat the rugs and rearrange them; without such regular care, the rugs may grow damp and rot. She shifts restlessly in her golden chair, robes the same fine softness as the rugs, the same shining gold as the intricately worked throne itself.

And she realizes with distress that she is *lonely*. How can she be lonely here, amid the sun and air?

No sooner has she registered the feeling than an attendant comes; Anna, a black-haired, pale-skinned woman with a pleasant face and great dark eyes. Sheanna knows her past and secrets, as she knows all her people. The woman enters the sanctuary and makes the necessary prostrations; she lights fresh incense in the golden dishes at each side of Sheanna's throne.

Sheanna favors her with a warm smile. But despite the warmth she feels for the woman, a coldness pervades the back of her mind.

Something is unsettled deep within her. Something is changing. And the Divine is not *supposed* to change.

She remembers the evolution of the animals. The mutation that allowed organic life to host intelligence: a long-awaited fruit of Earth. She did not guess the worth of that gem when she made it. Only the forces of time and randomness could make things that were new to her, and on Earth they had.

She remembers the little spaceships, metal-cased seeds scattered across the stars. Remembers the choice to split: one Divinity into many gods, to give the humans the companionship they so craved.

Sometimes still she speaks with her sister, dozens of

light-years away, the mistress of an ice world where human culture takes shapes that Sheanna finds fascinating. Her sister's is a world of cold, harsh beauty, of strange things the likes of which her own soil won't permit.

But she does love the spindly black trees and the turquoise sky and the sun, a burning copper penny like the ones the humans use for simple trades. She loves the silver grasses and the silver fish and the little brown birds, imported with the humans from their homeworld, who peep and make such wonderfully sweet music like that of the native whistling salamanders.

She loves the humans, most of the time.

Who could *not* love the young parents who bring their babes to her for blessing, whose illnesses she cures with a touch or a ritual to redirect the laws of the Void?

Who could not love the young couples who come to her, eyes shining with their mutual desire, to propagate their species with her blessing?

Yet she finds herself more and more these days *resenting* these little ones, who have what she never could. In their small, finite worlds, they have each other.

Sheanna is alone.

She has never seen loneliness in the mind of her sister, queen mother of the ice-world. She has never seen a trace of any such thing in any other deity. And that precisely is the problem. There are other divinities, but who can share her loneliness as the humans share their love?

She cannot, cannot be more like the humans than like her divine siblings. Such a thing would be impossible.

The humans tell tales of laughably made-up gods making love to mortals; these are symptoms of the mortal lust for perfection.

And yet—must all of those tales be entirely wrong?

Sheanna wonders, as she blesses another young couple with shining eyes, if a Goddess can commit blasphemy.

———

"Something has gone off," the handmaiden Anna whispers. "Have you noticed?"

"Off? Off how?" the servant named Rachel returns.

"She stares. She sits for hours in the sanctuary, staring. She used to hate staying in there unless it was required. She'd always be out among the fields and the flowers."

Sheanna has been wandering the halls, to quell her restlessness. She grew tired of gazing upon her own perfect form in a mirror after her lavender-scented bath, grew curious about the servants' quarters and whether their lives are like her own. So she has wandered, silent as air and desiring to make herself unseen, until she heard these voices.

"I thought perhaps she was maturing."

"I'm concerned," comes Anna's voice.

"What did it look like," Rachel asks, "when the others went wrong?"

A long pause. "Like this."

And for the first time in her memory, Sheanna is afraid.

She was not afraid when creation blazed into being with violence and chaos that has not been seen since; why should she be afraid now? She knows that her fear is foolish, knows that this is *wrong*. Knows that the immortal Divine of which she is a spark fears nothing.

But neither does the immortal Divine lust after human company. Neither does it *resent* the creatures it has nurtured so lovingly into existence. There is something wrong with her. Even the handmaidens see it.

This is more frightening than any death.

She looks back, back to the first fires of creation, seeking some resolution to her troubles. But she finds no answer there. If anything, looking back upon this ancient story makes her feel more wrong. More separate from what she once was. The mind now contained within her animal form does not match the mind that sparked those fires.

She returns to herself to feel the flaw still very present, spreading like a crack in her mind.

When the others went wrong.

Sheanna cannot ask her handmaidens, for deities never ask mortals for knowledge; it is the mortals who ask the deities. Yet she finds she does not know of whom or what they speak. How is this possible?

What is wrong with her?

She cannot ask her sister or the other entities among the stars, for their confusion would only make her panic worse. What would *they* do, confronted by a flawed god?

There is another, less rational reason she cannot ask them; she cannot name it just yet. Sheanna is beginning to feel another human emotion.

She is beginning to know shame.

Marcus comes to her in the dawn of his thirtieth year, and asks her blessing on his decision to take holy orders.

The relief that wells up within her brings with it greater shame. She will never have to marry this man to another woman.

To any woman. Sheanna is not a woman, and is shocked to have thought of herself as such. She is not of this body at all; rather, these bodies are of *her.*

Marcus bows before her throne with the other initiates, fifty of them filling the room. Their scratchy robes of plain brown burlap are a sign of their devotion. These new priests shall act as her emissaries wherever humans dwell on this world, and she pretends she has good reason to post Marcus here, with her.

He sacrifices for me, she thinks. Feels it not as the Divine, but as a woman.

Knows that she is slowly and inexorably going mad.

In an eyeblinks' time he will be dead, and perhaps then the madness will pass.

The thought causes anguish like a knife in her chest, and Sheanna looks down to see if she is bleeding. An eyeblinks' time will bring a worse madness, she now knows, but resolves not to let it show. Whoever heard of a deity in mourning?

This should be as easy as breathing, but it's not.

She wonders whether she could make him live forever. Knows this would be a crime against order too enormous to contemplate. Knows it could bring the destruction of all.

Yet still she wants to do it.

They need me to perform my duty. She looks out across the sea of prostrate heads. Tries not to single out Marcus' for attention.

They need me to be here, aloof.

What will happen if Sheanna leaves her throne?

What *does* happen when Divinity goes mad?

Sheanna is sitting on the soft silver grass at the banks of the stream behind the temple. The breeze is gentle and the air is warm and sweet with the thousands of scents of the forest.

She is holding a little salamander in her hands. The thing is too primitive, too low to communicate with divinity directly, as yet. It knows her only as a larger being, sees her beautiful long-fingered hands as a terrifying predator's jaws.

The tiny salamander's heart races in the way that humans' do when they are afraid, and it struggles to escape her grasp.

She begins to peel it.

The milky blue blood of her world's native life, copper-based, runs sticky down her hands. Human blood is red and thinner, she knows, and suddenly resents the humans for being different from this life, for being not her own.

"My Lady?"

It is Marcus' voice.

She is frozen to the spot. Begins to realize that she has committed a crime. Knows that divinities do not torture, do not kill, throws the writhing thing away from herself in horror. Feels herself falling as though the ground has disappeared. No longer knows what she is but feels that somehow, she is not Divine.

Her hands are shaking and her face a mask of naked terror.

Marcus' faith is shaken. She is right; a goddess should not be cruel or afraid. He stands as though frozen.

But where the goddess has vanished from view he sees a woman, and goes to one knee kindly as he would beside any woman in distress.

"My Lady," he says carefully, "what troubles you?"

Great violet eyes turn up to meet his. The eyes that have inspired awe in millions are like a child's eyes now.

"Marcus," she says faintly, "I think that I am going mad."

This doesn't make sense and it doesn't fit his theology, but how can one doubt the word of the Goddess herself? He will meditate on the troubling meaning of this scene later; perhaps it is a test for him.

For now, he lays a hand on her arm. It is an unthinkable breach of protocol for which he half-expects to be struck dead; but she looks as though she needs it.

Her arm is trembling, and as warm as any mortal's.

"How can I help?" he asks her.

She shakes her head, but seems grateful for his touch. "I do not know."

That evening, she wishes herself not to be seen and follows her handmaidens into their quarters again.

She must know how human women live. She must. She is not a true woman and can never be. She has seen how humans are. If she became one, with her power—there would be casualties.

And yet. And yet, what is she? How can a divinity be broken? Brokenness is supposed to be an attribute of chemical life; of things run on physical processes, not on perfection.

Divinity should not be able to malfunction. There should be no mechanism for it.

And yet she follows her handmaidens into the back of the temple, past doors of woven reeds and curtains of fine silk. Watches, invisible and silent, as her servants brush their hair, strands of it coming out in the brushes they use. As they doff their robes revealing flawed, imperfect bodies.

"How do you think she is holding up?" one of them asks the other, pulling night robes loose around herself.

"Better than expected, after the early signs. Still, I fear we'll have to replace her soon. There may have already been a breach. Brother Marcus came in today looking as though he'd seen something horrifying. He wouldn't tell me what troubled him. But he'd been down by the river, in her favorite place."

The other pauses. Sheanna recognizes a look of great sadness on her face, and the sound of a heavy sigh.

"Must we? Truly?" It is a sound she knows well; the sound

of parents who have lost a child to some freak accident that not even Sheanna could prevent, the sound of a human whose deep irrationalities make them not *want* to do what they must and commend the body to the ground.

"It's too much of a risk not to," the other says. "It could go very badly if we don't."

The handmaidens resign, quite unhappily, to sleep.

She does not know what possesses her to take the keys from the secret place where the handmaidens store them.

She has known for centuries that it was her solemn duty to pass on the keys to those who serve her in the highest capacities. But she has never wondered *what* the human-made keys unlock. It seemed unimportant. Now she searches for an answer in her infinite store of knowledge, and finds she does not have it.

She must know.

All the buildings on her world were built by humans, for her world's native life had no need of artificial shelter. The keys open her temple sanctuary, yes, and her private taber-nacle quarters. And the servants' own quarters, and some assortment of closets wherein the supplies for her rituals are stored.

But there are far more keys here than she has ever seen in use. What else do they open?

Sheanna herself has never walked all the corridors of her sacred city. She has never desired to, never been beckoned to it by the humans who built the city. And before the humans there were no cities, only earth and wind and grass and crawling things whose minds barely shadowed consciousness.

Now, she feels alone as she walks. Out of place. She is not

properly divine, anymore; she is not, cannot be human. She is not of the little salamanders who crawl beneath their orange Sun.

What is she? Are there none like her?

She is a child of the Void, a child of herself. Yet she is not animal; is not Divine. She is losing knowledge. Perhaps she never had it. Perhaps she was made defective.

That, somehow, is comforting. Then it would not be her fault.

There are so many things about the humans she has never bothered to ask. She has cared for them, and advised them in the ways of her world. They have worshipped her and venerated her. She knows the innermost workings of the human body better than any human ever could; and with her knowledge she can cure their diseases with a touch.

Their minds had seemed simple and not at all mysterious to her. Nothing that she needed to understand.

Nothing that she needed to understand, until she began to feel irrational herself.

Now, feeling irrationality from the inside, she wonders with trepidation what secrets her holy city holds. What have the humans built that she had never bothered to learn about? What secrets have they hidden from her?

Does she *want* there to be secrets? Does she want to be finite, small, capable of being wholly encompassed by their world?

She walks the hallways silent as air, not wishing to be seen. Holds the keys tightly in one hand, silencing vibrations. She walks deeper into the bowels of the temple than she has ever been before.

She passes her own quarters, vast and beautiful. Passes many rooms whose many purposes are known to her. Rooms devoted to the silent meditations of the monks and nuns; rooms devoted to initiations, to dreams, to healings. Rooms devoted to storage of the sacred grain and beer, to the preparation of the ceremonial feasts. Rooms devoted to storage of linens and candles and herbs.

At the end of the hall, for a moment she knows disappointment. The rooms she knows continue until she comes up against a stone wall, intricately carved with a depiction of the creation of this world. It is Sheanna herself who holds the sphere with its continents in one hand, overseeing it with an artist's delicacy, a mother's love and a lover's mystery at once. Her robes are inlaid with gold in the carving as in reality, while the copper sun shines bright and furious before her.

That creation, she remembers. The carving of this wall, she does not. She stares at the frieze, wonders how she has no memory of seeing it before.

Wait—the outer edge of her own body in the engraving is no mere impression in the rock. It is a seam, deeper than the other lines.

Sheanna looks down at the keys in her hand; back up at the image of her as creator-goddess. Will one of these keys open the hidden seam?

Yes! The slight part between the lips of her engraving hides a small, dark hole. She tries a dozen keys in it before one clicks and turns.

And the whole stone image of her body sinks back into the wall, recedes, silent as a whisper, to reveal a dark passage behind the wall in the rough shape of *her*.

Sheanna steps inside.

She has not been in total darkness since the beginning. On her land, the moon and the stars always give enough light for her to see. She finds it thrilling and revels in that which is beyond rare: the sensation of something ancient and new. She walks a few meters without sight, fingers trailing along the rough wall of the passage for guidance, until—

until the floor disappears from under her and suddenly she

is falling—

A brief fall and an undignified tumble, down stairs of stone like those at the temple's front. She manages to stop herself a dozen steps down by splaying hands and feet out to wedge between the walls of the staircase. Dizzy and disoriented, she stops to evaluate herself.

She feels no pain. She can't. Her body works as before. It is not designed to break.

But the fall disturbs her. Why couldn't she sense what lay ahead? Why was she not able to stop the fall through sheer force of will?

Surprise is no excuse—she has always been mentally prepared when performing miracles, this is true, but the Divine should not need preparation to work magic. The laws of physics themselves *should* be hers to control.

Is she only, only becoming human? What a relief that would be. She could live a lifetime as a human. Better that than as a mad god.

Uneasy now with the darkness, she creeps to her feet again. Raises a hand, and wills it to radiate light.

In the sudden-sharp light of her handheld sun, she sees that the stairs continue downward for a dozen meters. This takes her well below ground level. Sheanna glances back up the stairs, into where the passage ends in blackness. Wonders if this is what humans feel when they feel fear.

Curiosity and pride are stronger than fear, if that's what this is, and she continues down the steps.

The bottom of the staircase looks like a solid wall, but now she knows better. The stone face is carved with intricate symbols whose meanings are unknown even to her. This bothers her tremendously. What secret language have humans made and hidden from the unwary gods?

She casts about her palm-light until she sees a pinpoint of blackness deeper than the surrounding shadows; a keyhole. Tries thirteen keys before one fits.

She wonders, as a door-shaped portion of the wall sinks into a recess, how often her human servants have come this way. How many things do they know that she does not? An unnatural bluish-gray light spills into the corridor where the stone has parted, revealing a burnished metal floor beyond.

She imagines Rachel and Anna walking with their same silent demureness, down this secret passage hidden even from their god. Feels anger rising at their secrets; she never asked to know about this, because she did not know that there was anything to ask about. Her subjects should have told her all their secrets; she has watched over them day and night, and now she feels betrayed.

Sheanna steps onto the cold metal floor, still barefoot, for gods have no need for shoes. Steps further into the light, looking down at herself to survey the damage from the fall. Her golden robes have become scuffed and smeared with rock dust in her tumble down the stairs.

She looks up and stops dead. Is filled for the first time with what the humans must call dread.

There is a box made of glass like a crystal coffin, surrounded on all sides by artificial lights in a dozen colors. The lights change and pulse at random, in patterns which she knows must convey meaning but which are inscrutable to her.

Sheanna is lying under the crystal coffin, connected to dozens of tubes and wires.

It is a perfect replica of her. No statue or engraving, this; the nude figure *breathes* as she watches, its brown skin as soft and perfect as her own, cheekbones as high, hair as dark. If those eyes were to open she knows that they would be her perfect violet, and the first thing she wonders is—

How many times?

How many times had they replaced her? *How* had they done it; what was this creature below the glass? What was *she*, a goddess with ten billion years of memories?

An object of human manufacture? How? And why? Were the handmaids only helping the Divine?

No. That is not what her memories tell her, what they show her. And that means her memories are false. All of them.

Sheanna crumples to her knees. And thinks of Marcus.

Marcus. Marcus. She can only think of Marcus.

Not more than a woman, some part of her mind thinks, piecing together a puzzle her conscious mind cannot yet comprehend. *Less. Less than an animal. A machine made by animals. To serve them.*

She remembers Creation with absolute clarity. Under the weight of such contradictory information, her mind threatens to fracture.

How much is true?

"Sheanna?"

It is Rachel's soft voice.

Sheanna opens her mouth but finds she cannot speak. It is not rage or shock that renders her mute. Something is going wrong inside her head, a clouding and a slowly-spreading paralysis.

"Oh, Sheanna." The small woman gathers her goddess in her arms, lays her stiffening form on the cold metal floor.

"Let her understand," Anna says, walking in from behind Rachel. "She deserves that."

"She won't remember this tomorrow." Crystal tears fall from Rachel's eyes.

Anna crouches to lean over Sheanna's face and tells her:

"We have always needed gods. When we found none in the Void, we made our own. Only the godmakers know. The others can't, or they will be deprived of that which they need."

The part of her that remembers creation cannot believe this. She sees that part separating from her finite mind, her *self*.

"We tried to make you better than ourselves." Rachel tells her. Looks away from her goddess with red-rimmed eyes.

And then there is a third brown form kneeling over her, slanted violet eyes staring down at her. She knows the wonder that a worshipper must feel as a long-fingered hand reaches out and lays atop Sheanna's hair.

"You will not remember this," Anna promises, as though this is a comfort, as the new and uncorrupted goddess begins to copy memories from the old. The humans will edit out the broken ones, somehow, Sheanna is sure. How many of her memories, even of this lifetime, are her own?

How many times? she wonders, and wonders if Marcus will notice that she's gone. Changed. Replaced. Will he ever know?

A thousand other questions swarm within her mind, but there is no time for answers.

The walls that separate Sheanna from the Void fall like crumbling stone.

AFTER THE UPLOAD

"After the Upload" appears here for the first time following my stubborn refusal to cut 4,000 words off of it to fit into a professional magazine. I hope my stubbornness has been well worth it.

I remember how the Project began. Most everyone has forgotten, you know. They were all *there* for it, all except the netborn, but nobody paid much attention at the time and the myth they've painted is prettier. They like to think that they were all in on it, you see—participants in a conscious and concerted drive toward utopia, supported by the vast and unanimous network of humans around the globe.

The truth is that almost no one gave a damn about our work and those who did mostly didn't understand it. We were financed by a jury-rigged combination of defense and medical grants, scraping the bottom of the funding barrel and sleeping on the floors of our office when grant submission season came.

In those days I never believed we'd accomplish anything approaching our end goal in my lifetime—but I did not complain about funding.

One year, somebody read my application and saw fit to move me from an ancient little lab in the back room of a state college to an enormous facility near Washington, D.C., and put a lot of money at my disposal. With funds came overseers—from among both the military and the rich, many of them the same people who would support us while wearing, sometimes literally, different hats.

This is how a typical sponsor's visit to our laboratory went:

"How is the project going today, Remy?" One of the few dozen white-haired politicians who I could not tell apart, even then, would ask me. (The "P" in "Project" had not yet become capital, because we had not yet succeeded.)

At that point, mostly, we'd given some pretty good entertainment to about a dozen monkeys who were the precursors to human subjects. They seemed to quite enjoy playing with little balls that only existed in the computer matrix, and being rewarded for completing their tasks with little squirts of fruit juice. Peach juice was their favorite.

"We're making progress!" I'd enthuse, even if we weren't. Funding for pure research was scarce, scarce, scarce in those days, so you never let the sponsors doubt the inevitability of a return on their investment. You told them that they would get it in such great spades that they would invest more, and then be forced to conclude that they *had* gotten something back out of pure cognitive dissonance.

I'd show our visiting financier some neat little computer representation of a monkey and tell them things we weren't really sure of, about how the Bio monkey in the next room was controlling the computer-monkey, about how you could see by the way it batted its tiny hands that it could really feel the virtual ball being mapped onto the sensory cortex of its brain by the electrodes, about how if we pressed *this* button then the monkey would feel cold and wet for a moment (people liked to press that button and watch the monkey shiver, and feel like they had done something complicated and important).

The financiers' eyes would glitter. "How long until it's ready for people?" they would ask.

And I would always joke: "Well, you could be one of our first test subjects."

We managed not to kill anyone during the first tests, I think. So much is fuzzy now, blurred and indistinct, but I think I would remember that. I was always pathologically conscientious, from an early age—a genetic thing, probably.

Yes, that kind of thing was originally genetic. Hard-coded, too. You couldn't edit it at all until CRISPR came along. Sounds odd, doesn't it, not being able to rewrite your own source code?

At any rate, I don't remember any of the crippling fear or guilt that would have come from killing somebody. Don't look at me like that. I like to forget that you people find the concepts of guilt and fear *unpleasant*.

I do remember the first person we saved. It was Amelia Langley—yes, *that* Amelia Langley.

She was a young girl when I met her, fifteen years old and dying of leukemia (now there's a scourge I don't miss). She was cognitively sharp as a tack, neuroplastic as anything, and had nothing left to lose.

And she was also some defense contractor's daughter,

which meant she got to talk to us, while the thousands of other children dying of leukemia did not.

Don't look at me like that. None of that was my doing. It's not my fault if I remember it, or if I won't let the rest of you forget.

I'm sure you've seen her. She is little different now than she was then. Older, of course, in both brain state and appearance. But she always had red hair and green eyes (though she'd lost all her hair when I met her—I'll explain later). She always had a curious face and an even curiouser resistance to terror. And there were many things to be terrified of, in those days.

It was less hope and more curiosity that lit up her face when I spoke to her the first time. I was shaking in my boots at this new thing, this dying human who had been entrusted to me. She seemed at peace, the adult in the room between the two of us. I'd been told to reassure her, I remember, but it went more the other way.

We put the crown on her head, punched a hundred tiny holes into her skull and extruded a dozen tiny probes into each hole. And then we put her under—yes, the brain was in the head, remember? You know that. You'd just forgotten the implications of it. At any rate, the head was the access point for Upload—the only body part that really counted.

Amelia said that the sensations were funny. That was probably an understatement, judging by her bewildered expression when we bought her back up. But afterwards she smiled at the wire leads trailing out of her skull and caressed them, and I knew we had something, and it frightened me.

Amelia was the first complete Upload, error rate 0.6%. Unacceptably high today (philosophically speaking, maybe always?), but damned incredible for mid-21st century tech.

The program in the computer was Amelia, give or take 0.6%. It was missing part of her sense of humor, maybe, or her bitterness over her first boyfriend breaking up with her a year ago, or a few memories of the little spotted dog that used to come with her to the clinic as a comfort animal. It's hard to say what was missing, but what was *there* in the computer was beyond incredible—

99.4% of Amelia!

The principle of the thing is as basic to you now as the first words a toddler speaks, as why-wouldn't-that-work as gravity. But to us then, it was new.

It is impossible, I have discovered, to explain to a netborn what life was like Before. That humans could only exist within a big, squishy pile of waterlogged chemicals, cells and chromatin and ions, and that the *slightest* perturbation could destroy a brain—resulting in the irretrievable loss of consciousness and personality—in a matter of minutes.

The trouble is, of course, that you all have forgotten death. "Irretrievable" isn't a word we use around here much. It's certainly not something that happens to people. Except—

We'll talk about that later.

I used to see stroke patients when I was on medical rotation in my youth. Those were people who lost memories and abilities due to chemical disruptions of the brain. Some only limped a little. Others couldn't walk or speak. Yes, *permanently*. They couldn't just Upload then—not yet.

I remember watching them. Wondering, as seconds passed, just how badly their blood flow was compromised, how many neurons would die and explode, scattering their information into a senseless chemical stew that could not be reconstructed.

I'd wonder how many tiny parts of what had once been the person—memory, emotion, ability—would be lost before we could get blood flow re-established to supply the precious oxygen that allowed those superbly fragile bio-computers to continue to exist. If something was lost in those days, it was lost forever. Not intentionally, not carefully, but accidentally and all the time.

That wasn't how I thought about it then, of course. Computers were still devices for entertainment, not medicine. Doctors didn't even yet understand the delicate interplay that neurons depended on to stay alive. Certainly nobody could conceive of a day when the two would integrate and we would look back and ask 'what the hell was *that*?' about both of them, primitive flesh and metal alike.

Today we can understand those things, and we can ask that, but I'm not entirely sure it's a net gain.

Hypocritical, I know. I accepted the Upload's gift of immortality myself, and have not yet relinquished it. But I bear some responsibility for this reality; and so, some I have responsibility to be concerned.

There is a great deal you've forgotten, all of you.

Let me begin to explain why I am not always glad that we succeeded—and how I came to be where I am today.

Saving Amelia was a good thing. It was a great, unprecedented victory. The little girl's body expired but the contents of her nervous system remained alive and lively, controlling a pretty little computer simulation that had her green eyes and her round face until she decided, a few months in, that a more mature look suited her.

Dozens more sick children followed—children of the wealthy, all of them. Then it was sick adults, and then finally seniors. The first included not a few of our funders who had been counting down the days to human trials and hoping that their pacemakers didn't give out in the interim.

One of the men who had given us generous sums after learning about the Project through a defense department friend was 103 years old when we Uploaded him. Which I suppose means nothing to anybody, now, since most of you have been around for a couple of centuries, but in those days living past 100 was a rare feat.

I suppose I'm not making my case for the Bio world very well.

Had you heard of Erik Chiyari before—well, you know? That's probably good—you're far too young for his work. He was an artist, they say. And I won't deny that what he did could be called art, although it's the kind of art that would have gotten you a few centuries' worth of prison time back in the old days.

Yes I *know* I just said that people didn't live that long back then—it was a point the court systems would make, back then, to state intent to punish someone for longer than they could possibly live—

Never mind.

Suffice to say that if Erik Chiyari had come to me as a biological human living outside the Net, I would not have Uploaded him. Not if I had known about his work, his "art" and the impact it would have.

His work is considered perfectly harmless now, while I am not—*there's* a perspective change for you. Well, for me. And for those who remember.

Erik painted with blood, you see. *Actual* blood. Not Bio, physical stuff, of course. But he built his subjects simulated Bio skins, right down to the cell structures and the DNA. They were as perfect replicas of living matter as have ever existed in here, not the usual avatars coded only for aesthetics. You could probably have built a real person out of those skins, back in Bio space, if you had a printer good enough. In a way he was doing precisely the reverse of what I'd done.

He'd build those skins, as close as I've seen in centuries to real human bodies. And then he'd destroy them.

The ultimate homage, the critics said, to a biological past where anatomy and chemistry sustained life. The ultimate expression of humanity's triumph over death. His victims experienced violent death, but they did not die. They'd make public appearances with him a few days after the event, smiling, but somehow changed.

He sold copies of everything. In his own suite of programs, his experience and his victims' were both recorded. Audios and visuals and tactile reproductions were available. *Are* available, I suppose. Do you know anyone who has one?

'An homage,' they said. 'A celebration,' they said. But this is the kind of man Chiyari was: I visited his house once. He had about half a dozen human skins hanging on the walls of his house. And he sold replicas of *those* too.

And nobody dies of cancer anymore. But now people like Erik Chiyari cut people up for a living and hang their skins on his walls, and art critics praise his commentary on the human condition.

I'm not sure it's a net gain.

I remember the day Amelia invited me to her home. I was not prepared for what she wanted to tell me.

The sesquicentennial—*our* sesquicentennial, was approaching. Amelia was one-hundred and sixty-six years old, but had been choosing to appear around forty for the past century and a half. The age seemed to suit her—she'd had enough suffering in her brief Bio life to age most people fifty, but she had retained her youthful spirit.

By now, I had known her for a very, very long time as a woman ripening toward middle age. She was red-haired, green-eyed, round-faced with a mother's smile. I always wondered about that, as she'd never had any children in either the "new" or natural ways.

She greeted me with the warmest of those smiles as her front door opened, revealing Amelia and the scents of home.

It was one of those moments where, for me, awareness becomes boggled. I could not believe that the rough-grained oak of the door beneath her fingers was simulated, that the sunlight refracting off of it was not real, that the salt smell of the air and the faint dampness of the sea breeze was an illusion—

No wonder so many people forget. If my first memories of Amelia had not been so stark, would I still remember how things once had been? Would I *understand* with real immediacy, if my first life's work had not been to rage against the worst the Bio world had to offer?

"Come in."

For a moment I was overwhelmed by the memory of my own Welcoming, when I had been Uploaded with perhaps months left on my biological clock. Amelia's was the first face I saw here. Most of the others present were my patients from the previous half-century. It was enough to make an old man cry, back then, that they were healthy and alive.

And I realized, as I followed her into the entranceway of her home, the reason for my *deja vu*. Many parts of her home's design were *de novo*, concocted from some of the infinite array of settings and items available to any who should want them. But others, like the door and the hardwood floor that now made harsh tap-tap-tap noises beneath my feet, were taken from her father's house.

Her family had invited me for dinner almost weekly as our project neared its end. Amelia's Upload was poised to be, for them, as much a goodbye as a possible salvation. At the time, she was going where they could not follow; and we were not entirely sure the path we'd made for her was safe.

Then, suddenly, I knew who Amelia was modeled after. Why her form was so familiar. She looked like her mother—acted like her too.

And as we rounded a corner into the kitchen, I half-expected to see emaciated Amelia in her wheelchair with the little spotted dog wagging his tail beside her.

"Can I take your coat?"

I smiled and gave it to her, felt a certain emptiness as I did so. I'd spent almost a century of life taking pains to hide the actions of an anxious body—racing pulses, cold sweats, nervous twitches. Some part of me still expected that it should be difficult to hide my thoughts. But my programmed body bent to my will more easily than my Bio one would have. The vertigo from my trip down memory lane had vanished, simply because I wanted it to. I wasn't sure I liked that.

Amelia is a therapist now, dealing with problems I can't imagine. She works with patients' personality code directly, rewriting to achieve the effects they desire.

I thought, briefly, about submitting myself to her for a tune-up.

On this day, Amy seemed to know exactly what I needed. The coat-hanging ritual grounded and centered me. I savored the rough-yet-soft fabric of my tweed jacket—another wave of *deja vu* washing over me as I did so. She took it and hung it with care, as though there were a real possibility that it might crease if treated roughly.

"Hello, Amelia."

"There's tea," she said, and led me into her kitchen.

The spotted dog—*a* spotted dog—was pacing there, its little nails making click-click-clicks against the maple floor. I watched it debate how to parse the arrival of this new human in its domain.

"Is that...?"

"No," Amelia said softly. "I wouldn't put a Bio animal through this."

The almost-dog was friendly and endearing without overbearing. It circled me a few times before finally stopping and offering its snout to sniff my hand. I let it go.

Amelia looked over from where she was pouring iced tea, beaming. "His name is Trevor," she said. "He's a little shy around strangers, but he'll warm up if you want him to."

"He's beautiful, Amy."

I sat down in a spindly oak chair, and the silence stretched between us for a moment too long. There was something waiting here—a subject she was reluctant to broach. I could feel it in the air.

She brought a plate of lemon cookies to the table, and set them down before she spoke.

"Have you heard," she asked hesitantly, "of Erik Chiyari? The painter?"

Lack of an adrenal system be damned. My body, simulated or not, went rigid with alarm.

"Is...that what you call it, now?" I asked carefully.

"Yes." A note of defensiveness in her voice. "I do. I think what he does is beautiful."

I looked away. Watched her dog pace, nervously sniffing the floor where I had stood.

"I know this is hard for you, Remy."

My first name. Formalities observed, this was to be an adult-to-adult talk, then.

"You know *what* is hard for me?" I asked.

"Everything. So many things have changed because— because of what you've done. I wanted to make sure that you —had everything you needed."

I managed to meet her eyes. Felt the cold in my own, and hated it. But hated even more what I suspected she was going to say.

"I'm going to work with him on his sesquicentennial piece. It's—appropriate, don't you think?"

"Tell me you don't mean what I think you mean."

"Oh, alright; I'm going to *be* the piece, then. It's a perfect reversal, you see. Once, you saved me from a Bio body. Now I don't need one."

I found my eyes going strangely unfocused. Wondered if I could will *that* away, but found that I had no desire to do so.

"Does your father know?" The old man had been Uploaded even before me, a few months after his wife died suddenly of a heart attack.

"Yes," she told me. "But he has his own life now. And I'm —not particularly interested in anybody's feedback. I just wanted you to hear it from me. Not from someone else."

The words hung in the air between us.

"How long?"

"We've been talking for months."

"'Talking.'"

"Remy, don't."

She looked at me and with the slightest change to her posture became forbidding, reproving. Almost scornful.

The situation warped in my mind; became absurd. And, for lack of any other response, I started to laugh.

She sat at the table, the cookie platter between her and I. Tapped her foot and leaned forward on her elbows, the picture of long-suffering patience.

"Please, Remy," he said softly. "Sometimes, being old-fashioned is harmless. This isn't one of those times. You can be upset if you want to be. That's only hurting you. But don't try to change *my* mind. I have considered this carefully."

"Amy," I said to her. "Amy."

She waited.

"Doesn't it bother you that strangers will pay to watch him kill you?"

"I've been to Erik's shows."

Erik. She was on a first-name basis with the bastard, spoke of him with more than a little bit of affection.

What had I done when I killed Death?

"What scares you about this?" she asked me.

"What?"

"Bear with me. It's a therapy technique. What scares you, about me going to Chiyari?"

I flapped my mouth at her soundlessly.

"I know you've always been conservative, Dr. Burnes. I'll admit that surprised me at first, because you were all on the leading edge—back then. You were doing what others were afraid to even speak of.

"But your conservatism doesn't bother me anymore. I just..." she hesitated, "I wish you were happier here."

As she said it, a salted breeze stirs the curtain in the window nearest me. I was touched. Moved, nearly, to tears.

None of which helped my reaction to the thought of what Chiyari is going to do to her.

The window that the breeze was coming through looked out on the sea. I imagined that all four walls of the house did, because Euclidean geometry does not matter here. It's the same view I had coming in the front but from a different angle, jade whitecaps crashing with distant majesty on the rocks perhaps a hundred meters below Amelia's mountain perch.

I peered down at the whitecaps, the jagged black pumice rocks bare of such softness as grass or soil. I imagined the body-shattering—*irreversibly* shattering—power of ocean, sky and rock in the Bio world. I remembered how sunlight could bring cancer to unprotected skin, which could spread to other organs, how in the Bio world the Earth's fragile atmosphere was—is—surrounded by the void of space will suffocate or freeze you and will sometimes send asteroids hurtling out of the sky.

"I'm sorry, Amy," I told her. "I'm sorry if I have upset you." I hesitated, but could not resist: "You know it's going to hurt, don't you?"

"Of course it will. That's the point."

I flinched a little at the matter-of-factness in her voice, still strongly patterned after the voice of the Bio teenager I knew once upon a time. I wondered when Amelia Langley became so *bored*.

"But it won't change anything. Not in a bad way." She put down her cup of tea which, I suddenly noticed, had transformed from an iced glass into a steaming porcelain cup at some point in the course of our conversation.

"You made sure of that. I'll always exist. Until the explosion of the Sun or the heat-death of the Universe, anyway. And we have people working on solving those."

And I saw little Amelia, bald, gaunt, curious Amelia overlaid atop this eldritch creature who would lie down on Chiyari's canvas in a few short weeks, and I shook my head.

"I knew that old age involved confusion," I told her. "But I never imagined it would hold this much."

She smiled at me. "I wondered why your self-image remained old. So few people's do."

Her observation made me frown. To feel that you are old —not due to biological inevitability, but *willfully* outdated—is unsettling.

Amy was still smiling.

I began, that day, to notice new things about her. It had never been odd, to me, that a teenager would choose to look forty at sixteen—especially one who had faced mortality as brutally as Amy had.

But I had never noticed the particular attributes of Amy's chosen form. Things that had always been there in her forty-year-old body-design, in the thickness of her lips and the darkness of her lashes and, somehow, in the sharpness of beginning wrinkles at the corners of her eyes and mouth.

How much of this woman did I never see before?

Was she a woman, frozen like the rest of the world in my mind—or had I stunted her maturation when I copied her neural patterns into code?

"Why do you *want* what Chiyari's offering?" I asked, looking for a way for this to make sense.

And I saw the horrible beginnings of heat behind her eyes. "Death. You took that from me when you moved me here. I don't regret that I will stay alive. But there are experiences that—a person should have."

She could make this thing sound almost sane.

"Besides," she said, "he's an artist."

Oh dear, sweet Jesus, I thought, *what is wrong with the world?*

The world that I made. The world I had constructed for her, for all of them.

Amy was attracted to this butcher. I didn't build *that*.

I caught myself thinking that *maybe* I would have left that part of her out, let it die with her cancer-riddled flesh. If I had known what she contained, if I could have changed that without changing her too much…

'*In a system as interdependent as a mind,*' a line from an old textbook comes back to me, like an ugly nursery rhyme, '*to change a single aspect is to change the entire system.*'

Amy's green eyes remain on me, waiting, patiently, for me to understand. Panic grips me for no reason I can name, and she stares into space for another minute, her eyes glazed, *daydreaming.*

And suddenly I'm filled with a real murderous desire to kill this Chiyari fellow.

And I realize that that is not wholly outside of the realm of possibility.

Chiyari was netborn. He was never burdened by a biological body nor shaped by one, birthed instead by complicated algorithms that constructed his nervous system from the templates of other human minds.

This made Chiyari, technically, an AI—but considered legally human, as there was little enough difference between him and us now.

Almost all children for the past century and a half had been netborn. Bearing a child into a fragile, limited biological body had begun to be considered cruel very shortly after the Upload became accessible to all.

I think somebody arranged a biological birth as an art project a few years back. They had to use frozen sperm and eggs and robotic cloning vats to control the process from inside the computer matrix, because nobody thought far enough ahead to preserve a reproductively viable population *outside* the computer matrix when abandoning them entirely became possible. Well, people like me thought of it; but that, too, was considered cruel.

The baby was fine, or so the press coverage said—and I believe it. I remember well the perfect health of the vast majority of births I attended in the Bio world. Although I do wonder about the unforeseen effects on this poor baby, who was raised entirely by lovingly designed robots projecting holograms of his in-matrix parents for ten years before they decided to Upload him.

His life was a popular reality show for a while, I remember—considered both thrilling and controversial because the possibility of permanent death existed for him. Doing that to a child, the majority opinion soon held, was unthinkable.

Anyway. Chiyari was netborn. He was never subject to such cruelties as the possibility of death.

I began to research him. The first shock was that I knew his mother. From Before. I did not know her well, but she had worked in biotech a couple of centuries ago. She'd been an up-and-coming talent when I retired. I remember shaking her hand at a conference once, a mechanical nicety. I remember that there was something unsettling in her eyes. Later she'd asked questions about human subjects research that unsettled me even more.

She'd decided about half a century after her own Upload that she wanted a son. One that she could design, in every aspect, from scratch. She'd made a copy of her own brain—quite a brilliant brain, as I recall—and introduced the necessary changes to make it male. She upped the aggression factor because she had, by her own account, always felt herself too passive. Said in interviews, after her son gained fame, that she had always considered herself to be a pathological wallflower.

She'd added a bit of sensory-art appreciation—another thing she had always found lacking in herself. Added some witch's brew for sociability, wiped the memories clean, age-regressed the resulting neural pattern and placed it in a lovely little programmed baby body.

Voila. The result was a beautiful psychopath.

The young Chiyari played the violin and made 2D and 3D light sculptures until he was about twelve—at which point he started slicing up his own arms and was disappointed not to find anything interesting inside. So his mother began teaching him Bio anatomy and coding, to make himself a body that resembled the ones his Bio ancestors had had. Naturally.

She helped convince the others that he was a visionary—one of the few who understood how fundamentally the

Upload had affected us. That his art was simply something that enlightened people got used to, like programming babies from scratch, or interacting with people who've programmed themselves to have the bodies of centaurs at a dinner party.

After all, the rules of our world meant that the kid couldn't *actually* hurt anyone.

He killed his first volunteer victim—his first publicized one, anyway—when he was sixteen. The same age Amy had been when she Uploaded. A very different creature, the young Amy had been, from a world of Bio steepled roofs and white picket fences and sunlight and soccer matches and death, a world where people still protected their children because there were still things that couldn't be rewritten.

I'd had some thought, when I first started, of sharing my research on Chiyari with Amy. But I soon saw that that would be pointless—everything I found was public. Everything, likely, she had read already.

It became more about knowing what I was up against.

Now chronologically fifty-six years old—and spiritually probably about five. Chiyari had stopped his aging algorithm and inhabited a roughly twenty-six-year-old body, blonde- and blue-eyed like the one his mother had designed for him at birth.

The overall effect *was* charming. Even I had to admit that, watching his recordings. A winning smile, a face whose symmetry even I could appreciate.

I found that I hated the bastard.

I had to see Chiyari. I had to talk to him. It would have been a psychological necessity, even if it weren't a technical one.

The self-proclaimed artist was happy to oblige. There are

advantages to being one of the most famous people in the world—and when I wrote to him, he answered. His reply, written on lovingly programmed antique stationery, said in beautifully looping handwriting that he would be honored to meet me.

I held the letter a little bit away from myself after reading it. Found myself wondering at the politeness of it, wondering if Chiyari and I were already engaged in a game of cat-and-mouse. Or if I was being completely delusional.

The antiquated stationery—chosen by Chiyari for an antiquated soul like me? He'd never resorted to text in any of his other art or communications that I'd seen, except as a purely aesthetic ingredient in visuals. He'd written in blood once, I remembered, involuntarily—his own blood mixed with that of some other man, repeating some poetry written centuries before my own time.

His letter to me sung the praises of my work. Said in too-warm terms how much he owed me.

How much he owed me. If I had not done what I did, this creature would not exist. People would not buy his recordings, and—

Amelia would be dead, and how many others?

Someone else would have done it eventually, chimed an automatic voice in my brain, established long ago, originally as a guardian of humility. *This world, being possible, was always inevitable.*

Was it, though? I wondered and for a moment, before I managed to shove it away again, the weight of responsibility was crushing.

I wondered if Chiyari hated me. I could not see sincerity in his words. If he knew me well enough to send old stationery, did he know me well enough to predict my feelings about the sesquicentennial? To predict my reason for contacting him? Or did he truly assume that my intentions were pure?

You're getting paranoid, Remy.

Perhaps it was something else. Because I was the First Welcomer, after all. He could not learn about Amy without learning about me.

And suddenly, I felt ill.

I was the First Welcomer, the original conqueror of Death. Chiyari claimed that his every work was a celebration of my own.

Did he think I wanted to *help* with his show?

Whether he understood—or even suspected—that I might bear him ill will was perhaps the most unsettling question. It still is. Could he understand the protectiveness of a friend? Or was he a manner of creature so different that he *believed* all that he said about his art?

Perhaps his admiration, his apparent idolization of me, was genuine.

We all ignore our own uncomfortable possibilities. This is one of mine.

Chiyari was waiting for me in a stylish coastal cafe. The sensibilities of the 1940s and 50s were popular at the time, and this cafe fit that to a tee. The cobalt skies and jade seas near Amy's apartment were repeated here, along with white sugar sands and a charming recreation of a 20th century roadway complete with cars that may have been functional constructs driven by real people, or programmed pieces of scenery. There was probably a bit of both.

He was leaning lazily to one side in the cafe's white metal chair, wearing dark glasses against the sun's glare in an apparent effort not to break the cafe's vintage atmosphere.

The vintage effect was, however, ruined by the ten-foot-long wasp hovering at a table behind Chiyari, apparently conducting business negotiations with a fairy. It helped that the wasp seemed to have brought its own theme music, a metal ballad that emanated gently from its table.

I sat down between my quarry and the wasp, and tried to shut out the sound of heavy bass.

"Good Doctor," Chiyari gave me a truly brilliant grin, perfect teeth a clean yet respectably natural shade of ivory. He extended a hand and shook mine, warmly.

I tried not to stiffen at the touch; his flesh was warm and strong and *alive*, practically vibrating with enthusiasm. It might just be possible to like this man.

For some reason, that made me hate him more.

His grin lingered for so long I actually felt myself begin to feel flattered, a dangerous warmth that I permitted so as not to come across as suspicious. Not that any of these brilliant young things, my Amy or this Chiyari or the giant wasp behind me, are really afraid of anything.

Hell, if I attacked Chiyari he'd probably take it as a compliment.

I realized that Chiyari had withdrawn his hand, and I had not yet spoken. His brows were beginning to draw together into a concerned frown at my silence.

"Doctor Burnes," he said, before I could speak, "you seem troubled."

If I beat around the bush, I may never get the words out in the face of all this charm and horror.

"I want to ask you to call off your sesquicentennial."

He went still. Even the wasp's theme song and the conversation at the next table seemed to quiet. I thought I had upset the bystanders until I realized Chiyari had put a sound-dampening field around us. Something a netborn would do as second nature; something I'd forgotten I *could* do.

"I'm—I'm sorry?"

"It seems a…" I floundered, looking for words that would not make me seem hopelessly obsolete. "Distasteful way to celebrate my work." A pointed reminder that this *is* my work, all of it, and he should care what I think.

I found then that I didn't wholly *want* to kill him. But part of me did. My inner beast raged against my conscience for long moments. What would I do if he turned out, in spite of everything I'd seen, to be a decent person?

A long moment passed in which he seemed to be seriously considering my request. He looked ponderous, tapping one sharp cheekbone with a slender finger as he thought.

I wished he would spit venom at me, or drip contempt. I wished he would be the monster I'd imagined.

"I think," he said at last, "that I can think of no better commemoration than what I am offering. Amelia was the first to escape the certainty of biological death; she escaped it quite narrowly and bravely. I am sure that you remember this better than anyone."

He allowed a pause, as though genuinely expecting me to nod in agreement. Then he leaned forward, spread his open hands on the table. Amicable. Reasonable.

"This will be a recreation all the more meaningful for being performed by the original participant." He seems to hesitate. "I'd thought of inviting you to be involved, but I didn't think you'd want to be. When you asked for me here, I wondered if I'd offended you with that omission."

I made myself smile, without the anchor of biology to force me to look the way I felt. Nausea vanished at my request; the visible color of my face did not change, though I felt as cold as though it had been drained.

"I assure you, I am not offended that you didn't ask. But I am, if we are being honest, somewhat offended by the proposal itself. Death was not a thing to be laughed at when

Amy Uploaded; nor is it today. Just because it hasn't happened in a century or so doesn't make it any less terrible. The sort of thing you are proposing, in the Bio world—"

Chiyari leaned over the table, addressed me seriously. "I know. It would be awful."

That stopped me. And he stared at me for a long time, almost pitying, choosing his words carefully.

"You realize, of course, that this isn't *real* death? It's not death *at all* in any meaningful sense of the word. The degree of pain will depend upon Amy's preference, as will the length of interruption of her cognitive processes—if there is any."

I bit my tongue. Could not stand to meet his eyes.

"Not real death," I murmured. "Not permanent. But real death still exists. A thing which Amy, as you say, narrowly escaped. A thing which a great many of us worked very hard to prevent, and feared that we would fail. A thing which still could happen, despite all of our advances. We have not solved every problem."

Chiyari took a polite moment to consider this.

"But you did succeed with her," he reminded me. "You succeeded so thoroughly that death could not touch her now if it tried. Not by my hands, or any others'."

I felt a strange, silent glee at his clear sense of invulnerability. Felt less glee when I thought of Amy, and said:

"It could. Just because your hands won't accomplish it does not mean that it's impossible."

Chiyari seemed to be genuinely struggling to understand what I was talking about.

"And," I charged ahead, "what you do—it reminds the elders among us of other things, you know? There was a time when we had to fear that—predators—would steal our children away permanently, would end their lives in pain and fear."

"I am no predator," Chiyari said softly, in the tone of one mortally offended.

"I'm not suggesting that you are," I managed to say. "But artists have an infinity of choice as to their range of media. Must Amy's flesh be yours?"

Chiyari gazed seriously at me for another moment; then relaxed, smiled, and I saw some of the contempt I had been half-hoping for edging into the corners of his mouth.

"Doctor Burnes," he said softly, almost patronizing. "Have you never been to one of my demonstrations? Would you like to attend one, before the sesquicentennial?"

I shook my head and hoped the gesture managed to seem casual. "No. That won't be necessary. It's the principle of the thing I'm concerned about. The message you're sending."

"The message," Chiyari said smoothly, "is that the Universe is ours now. Nothing can stop us. Do you know the lengths I am going to have to go to, to create a body with arteries and veins for Amy? Red and white blood cells, hemoglobin, chromatin, platelets—did you know that I do those, too? Surely you know that blood no longer flows beneath your skin. My works are the only place you'll find those molecular structures in this world.

"That's the gift you have given us," he continued. "We no longer rely on oxygen to breathe, and so we can explore our universe for the first time. We're no longer slaves to programmed cell death, so we can undertake projects that will take centuries and expect to live to see their fruit. I know as much human biology, probably, as you do, Dr. Burke. That makes the two of us members of a very exclusive minority—artists. Nobody but artists care about such things anymore. Nobody has to."

I found myself looking at Chiyari with a very strange feeling growing in my stomach. His attempt to invoke a sense of kinship between us, revolting as it was, had not completely failed.

"I'll consider that," I heard myself say.

"Come by my studio sometime, Dr. Burnes," he urged me, almost fatherly, as he stood. "I think that it will set your mind at ease. You may find some of its elements refreshingly familiar."

In the space of an eyeblink I was back in my own living room without giving him the courtesy of a goodbye.

A week later, I sent him a netburst. Cordial, almost apologetic, no-hard-feelings-right?

His response started cool and then warmed, asserting the power of choosing-what-to-tolerate, then forgiveness, camaraderie, come-and-see. It was written on another piece of pseudo-aged stationery that materialized on my desk a few hours after I reached out to him. The invitation was also a door.

I could feel the little code wrapped up in it. As I opened it, I could feel beneath the space it occupied the way that the doorway would open. It would unfurl like a wormhole, and neatly pop me through onto Chiyari's turf when I asked it to.

I felt myself almost tingling with curiosity as I looked at it. What would the lair of a creature as inscrutable as Chiyari look like?

The wormhole blazed into existence amid a shower of sparks which swirled around me in a sudden, circular wind. All aesthetics, intentional and unnecessary touches. One thing I had to give this Chiyari, one thing we had in common —he was no utilitarian.

My surroundings faded to darkness, sparks still dancing in it.

When light returned I was standing in a glass-fronted apartment. The sparks burrowed into thick, soft burgundy carpet, disappearing.

At first, the most surprising thing about his home was the ordinariness of it. The place was sparse and stylish. Superficially, it could not have been more different from my own, but there was an unsettling similarity about it. Perhaps it was the arrangement of the furniture; perhaps it was an aura of privacy.

It had the huge glass windows that have always belonged to penthouses and artist's studios, but the view beyond them was not a skyline or a bustling street. It was a desert, as empty of observers as the bare wall in my own house.

The desert was a simulation of nature's palette of chocolate browns. A cracked plain strewn by rocks like ancient pottery shards with mountains in the distance. Behind the mountains, the sun was setting, blue and tiny. This uncanny light, I realized, accounted for the air of surreality in the apartment.

"It's beautiful, isn't it?" Chiyari said behind me. I whirled to face him, despite my intention to look nonchalant.

One of his golden eyebrows arched in amusement. Seeing his face half-hidden in the strange shadows didn't help my sensation of impending doom.

"It's Mars," he said, coming to stand beside me. "Real-time footage from a rover. Almost real-time; there's a seven-minute delay on the lightspeed signal. I rewound it to sunset so you could see. The dust in the air scatters blue light, amplifies it at dusk. It's the opposite of what Earth's atmosphere does."

I had no idea how to respond to that. No idea what any of this said about him. Everything about him seemed so staggeringly alien—and yet familiar, as though I felt I knew him very intimately despite our short acquaintance.

I looked desperately around the apartment for something innocuous to comment on, for something to say.

He had photographs on the walls, just like I did. His were black-and-white, another aesthetic callback to a lost age. With a chill, it occurred to me to wonder if this man may have become one of my colleagues if he'd been born two centuries earlier. Would I have met him in the lab, lived alongside him with no knowledge of his depravity? Would he have worked with me on saving Amy?

I shuddered to think what else he might have been.

"Your photographs are lovely," I told him, before my brain had fully processed the fact that the smiling people were probably his past 'subjects.' On the wall nearest me a woman wore a particularly coy smile, her face sharing a frame with a disturbing splatter pattern of wine red on white paper.

Chiyari's expression warmed. "Thank you," he said, and I tried to hide my remorse for the compliment.

"I—why Mars?"

Chiyari smiled, and this time there was a little remorse behind *his* grin.

"It seemed appropriate. We're not making way for biological life on the other planets anymore. It seemed as though— someone should be out there, you know? Or at least be mindful that they exist."

Suddenly he went still, a hushed expression I had not seen in many years. I realized what his expression reminded me of—it was the expression of someone who had been startled by the appearance of a wild animal, and who did not want to scare it away.

I followed his gaze, and my stomach lurched.

A horribly unnatural *something* was nuzzling at the Martian ground a simulated few feet from the window at my back—rooting at the packed dirt with a jagged muzzle and long, spindly legs that ended in sharp claws.

"That's not my work," he whispered, as though the thing might hear us and flee. "A collaborator—the Martian environment is the work of a small clique. I am one of their few clients. They populate it with simulations of what Martian life *may* have been like, had the planet's history taken a different course."

The black spindly thing seemed to have found something in the ground, and was gulping it down with deeply unsettling motions. I realized that I could hear it shuffling—perhaps the thing could also hear us, and perhaps it really *was* designed to run away.

As though in response to my thought, the *thing* raised its too-long head and fixed veiled black eyes on me. It froze, relaxing into a stillness that I was afraid to break.

Chiyari made a small movement and the Mars-deer bolted away into the desert, vanishing in the gathering night with unbelievable speed.

Chiyari exhaled as it left.

"Beautiful," he breathed. "Perhaps someday we'll make Bio copies of those things. They're talking about doing that, you know—designing some new species with your beloved biochemistry."

I was not sure I could take any more talk with this man I did not want to like.

"May I see your equipment?" I asked him. "I'm terribly curious about it."

He led me down a staircase made of glass and into one of the strangest places I have ever been.

In some ways, it was its very familiarity that made it strange. The place did not look like a laboratory, as I'd been half-expecting. His talk of fabricating hemoglobin, chromatin and the rest had me envisioning electron microscopes, genetic amplifiers and other pre-Upload-style pieces of equipment. Physical workings in black boxes, row upon row of metal/glass/plastic lenses and reaction chambers upon benchtops.

Instead, the room resembled a perfume shop.

There were shelves not unlike those that would have held sterile glass bottles in a lab—but these bottles were dizzyingly colorful. They were an array of softly feminine shapes, classical and modern colors, wild patterns. I imagined using these in my old lab: *'Hand me the fuschia-and-magenta one with the teardrop stopper.'*

The countertops themselves were rectangular and white —but half-covered by plants. The things grew seemingly out of nothing, out of the countertop itself, in shades of green interspersed here and there with a climbing vine in a dizzying shade of indigo or a vibrantly violet miniature tree.

Chiyari was walking among them, beaming with what I recognized as professional pride.

"I keep my constructed copies of the genes and cell types here," he explained, indicating one shelf. "Once upon a time I grew the cells in culture—a complete simulated metabolism, carrying out all of the necessary biochemical reactions and such in real-time. Took an unbelievable allocation of computing power, as I'm sure you can imagine. My mother's popularity is a good thing for my work—I was able to rent a couple of servers without too much trouble. But it seemed wasteful to continue. Now I keep the little things in stasis when they're not being used for a project."

He took down a vase made of pink-and-clear swirled glass, a matching glass stopper corking its long, straight neck. With deft fingers he removed the stopper and offered me a look into the container's mouth. A viscous, dark red fluid stared back at me.

"Red blood cells. Complete simulations, or nearly complete. Hemoglobin is one of my favorite molecules, and so neglected—but I included the cytoplasm, the cell membrane and all known proteins. Erythrocytes are easier to simulate fully than other cells. I'm sure you know that they require no DNA."

So they don't have to be custom-coded for each subject, I thought. Would Amy's simulated cells contain her whole Bio genome? I was sure that data was stored somewhere.

He replaced the stopper and put the thing back on the shelf, just as my skin began to crawl. He took a few steps to drag a fingertip along a rack of what appeared to be multi-colored test tubes.

"I told you that I do chromatin, too. I don't go *all out*, of course, but I like to approximate the concept. Building a full human genome would be incredibly laborious, but I have copies of a few thousand different personal identity markers —the DNA sequences associated with different hair colors, for example, different eye colors, different skin colors. I have sequences related to aspects of mood and personality, height and bone structure, sex, of course—and mitochondrial DNA associated with various ethnic groups and geographic locales.

"Many people here don't know their ancestry—isn't that odd? You paid such close attention to the structure of their nerves in the Upload, but almost none to the structure of their genes. That information may be lost forever, now, for many of them."

I realized as I listened that Chiyari was probably right. And he was probably a better biologist than I am. He may have been doing all of this for the sake of tearing human bodies apart—an interest I found revolting—but he was rapidly revealing an interest in the laws of the Bio world more genuine than any I had seen in decades.

He smiled fondly, and threw an almost involuntary glance towards what I suddenly realized was an enormous tank in the corner, covered by a black tarp. "You don't want to hear about the body I'm working on for Amy, probably. But if you do, I could show you..."

Images came to my mind of another Upload-world anachronism—the Mutter Museum, where bodies had been displayed in various stages of disassembly. The bodies had been donated at death by their original owners for the education of the gawking public. A disembodied nervous system, circulatory system, skeleton. A pair of eyeballs attached to optic nerves, staring at me through formaldehyde—

I declined.

Bowing to my sensibilities, he moved on.

He showed me a couple of light sculptures—chemical structures enlarged to show the physical forms of the genes encoding for red hair, green eyes, and porcelain-pale complexion. A few stylistic choices made the chemical structures wispy and organic, vibrating with Brownian motion. A stylishly enlarged molecule of hemoglobin was a web, a delicate and intricate crown cast in shades of pink and violet.

When at last the lights rose and the sculptures vanished, I had to admit that his work left me with a faint sense of awe. *Most* of his work; my eyes strayed to the tank against the opposite wall.

A new body for Amy. A new flesh-and-blood body with more rich complexities of Bio human life, probably, than any other currently in existence. A new vessel, breakable, mortal, but capable of what it meant to be *us* without the veil of control the rest of us Uploaded had long-since wrapped ourselves in.

A new body. This was the thing I could not give her a century and a half ago; I would have given her that instead of *this* if I could have, but I did not have the skill. Of course, I had not had Chiyari's tools either—the ability to synthesize any chemical or structure, simply by *knowing* how it worked.

If I'd had the ability, would I have given Amy a new mortal body instead of an immortal digital life? Would it have been better if I had?

If I had, perhaps no one else would have accomplished Upload in my lifetime. I would not be standing here in an apartment on simulated Mars, but Amy would have had a Bio life. A spouse and children, maybe, grown in her own belly. Inescapable hardships and victories that meant something.

Chiyari stopped to pet one of his plants on the way out; a venus fly trap of emerald and gold, which closed a thorned mouth on his finger when he prodded it. One of the spines pierced his skin and a ruby drop welled until he licked the wounded finger.

The significance of the action—that he was maybe the only person in my world who kept blood beneath his skin—was not lost on me.

"Thank you for coming, Doctor," Chiyari told me, genuine gratitude in his voice. "I hope you have enjoyed your visit. And I hope I will see you again."

A few days later I was back in the warmth of Amy's home, this time in the teal-carpeted parlor adjacent to her entry hall. This was a more intimate space than her kitchen—and, I sense, a more adult one. This was a place for work to be done.

We sat in cushioned Victorian-inspired chairs, drinking hot tea.

"I'm so glad you've come to peace with this, Remy." I was 'Remy' from the outset this time, an equal and a friend. I knew my smile betrayed none of my uneasiness as I watched Amy, rapturously graceful, lower her cup to its saucer.

"Yes," I said to her. "Things are different now. We must come to terms with that—accept what it means. Of course, I don't think we've even begun to figure that out. Chiyari and his—paintings—are probably representative of our new culture in its infancy."

Amy smiled at me warmly, with the air of one who's pleased with a student.

"Our society has existed like this for one-hundred and fifty years," she said. "There were empires in the Bio world that didn't last that long. But infant for our timescale, yes. Still in its infancy."

"There were also empires that lasted twenty times longer," I reminded her. "This sesquicentennial is nothing to the span of human history."

"You're right. It's not." Amy leaned forward, wrapped her fingers around her mug of tea as though to warm them.

"Were you nice to him?" she asked.

"To Chiyari? I like to think so."

She snorted, and I saw a teenage girl's giggle. Tried not to think of us as father and daughter, tried not to think of Chiyari as her date.

The moment passed as quickly as it came, and Amy was all maturity again.

"I worry about you, Remy. He said you seemed confused. Out-of-sorts. Are you..." I could feel her hesitation to offend, to approach me as a therapist rather than a friend. "...are you alright?"

Confused, yes. Out-of-sorts. That would be a good way to put it. But I would not let her worry for me.

"I was older than you when I was Uploaded, Amy. I still am. And you know I won't take those damned youth mods, so don't ask me to."

"Yes, Remy," she said sadly. "I know you don't like modifi-cations."

I wondered what she would do—what she would say, what she would feel—when she found out about the new thing I was planning to add to the world I brought her into.

I had not been completely idle in the century-and-a-half since my Upload.

I did not study new things with the voracity of Amelia and her ilk; had not engaged in the same sensory explorations, come to accept the same new truths, or fought to build a place for myself in this deathless society the way she has.

But I clung, with an old man's grasping, to what measures of control I could. Immediately upon entering this matrix, I had to know how to manipulate it. And though many functions of manipulating my environment would never be reflexive to me—the sound-dampening shields, the re-winding, the pretty little apps like Chiyari's wormhole or our giant wasp friend's body—I remembered enough about the pre-Upload world to ask the deeper questions.

The fundamental questions of a computer program: what is its language? Not 'what clever little shortcuts have other people built?' but 'how does the data interface with the machine at the bottom of it all?'

I sometimes felt like a ghost or a mystic, walking through my world. Like one of very few people who were even aware of the deeper truth, the *physical* devices we all lived on.

Perhaps that's why it worked. I asked not what magic words I must say, but what the magic itself was made of. I dug into the code of time and space, dug layers-deep until I hit cold silicon with a stream of binary numbers passing through it in the same way nerve impulses once passed through the human brain.

I dug *that* deep and learned to dive layers deeper than most netizens would. Under sensory perception; under the invisible communication streams and other 'sixth senses.' Underneath, even, the basic property-coordinate links and into the mother files that held the very essence, the ongoing process of a human mind. I saw through our existence, and *that* was where I made my changes.

I wanted to know the parts that only the programmers had understood on the day we uploaded Amelia. I learned how the people around me worked. Could have been a healer, perhaps, if there had not been a repletion of those. As it was I kept my talents to myself for a long, long time.

But for my newest project, I needed a test subject. I started with a copy of Chiyari's little flytrap.

My code capture program had worked its flawless magic on that construct while I visited Chiyari's home, locating its original server and lifting the necessary binary to recreate it in full. I stored the stolen record on my own server; activated it in my own bedroom and let it blossom.

Its development sequence had been included in the code, and I set it to run from start to maturity over the course of a week. The thing would blossom from a tiny lime-green shoot into an emerald-and-gold thing with leaves spread the radius of my hand and a stalk as tall as my forearm. And teeth. Teeth strong and sharp enough to cut the skin. I planted the seed of the thing in my desk.

Then I sat down to eat—a purely voluntary ritual—and waited.

I asked Chiyari to come see me when a week's time was up. A reciprocal invitation; a reciprocal opening of my home to him.

He smiled at me and insisted on offering his hand again—which nearly made me shudder again, his flesh so warm, alive, and solid-seeming. The confidence with which he leaned close to me told me he thought he was becoming part of my inner cadre. In another life, perhaps, he might have been.

Three visits from the great Remy Burnes—culminating in an invitation to the doctor's own home—must have been something that the younger netizens would assume was glamorous and rare.

Well, rare—I'd give them that. I couldn't actually remember the last time someone less than a century and a half old had been inside of my apartment.

He came in through the door, not by way of teleport—an old-fashioned sort of modesty on my part and perhaps a little bit of shame. I always made a point of keeping my place humble. Close to my roots. *Accurate.* None of these fantasy castles for me, thanks. I lived in a recreation of Old St. Louis, near the medical campus. I keep my streets accurately pedestrian and noisy and unwashed.

Chiyari actually looked concerned by the time he took in my living room—apparently his generation had missed the myth of the sage who keeps humble surroundings. He looked as though he may have been taking my living room with its stained carpet, tattered leather sofa, and sun-faded polaroids on the wall as a sign of mental illness.

"Please," I told him, "come in."

He obliged, with consideration but nothing like caution in his step. His eyes lit up with fascination as he realized that his shoes were actually tracking dirt from the outside, and for a moment I hated myself for what I had planned for him.

The spark of interest in something new passed quickly, as for any netborn, and he gravitated towards my photographs.

"These are very nice," he murmured. He eyed an old

polaroid of my wife and daughter—both deceased in a car accident a decade before I met Amelia—with entirely too much interest.

"They're not art," I told him.

"I know." There was something like reverence in his voice.

I wished he wouldn't show such reverence. Wished that he had not re-created Amy's body in such loving detail. Wished that there was nothing in this man that I could like.

I drummed my fingers nervously, imagining that I was twisting little lines of code in the air around me. I laid them around Chiyari in an intricate spiderweb-pattern. The web glowed faintly in my mind's eye, and something predatory flared in me.

"Now it's my turn," I told him, "to show you something new."

Chiyari blinked, wondering and unafraid, and followed me into my bedroom-office.

He took in the bed with more uncomprehending judgement of my lifestyle. Not comprehending that I should choose to sleep and work in the same space when infinity was available; a little confusion, perhaps, about why I was showing him such an intimate space.

Then he saw the flytrap on my desk, and his eyes went wide.

"You copied me!"

Copied, used in that sense, referred to a theft of intellectual property. But he sounded not at all displeased, and slightly flattered. "Did you know I wrote that program myself?"

"I suspected. Watch."

And now I pulled the string that starts the cascade around the little flytrap, the test-run of the program I'd been working on for the past three weeks.

The little flytrap was gone. As though it never existed. Simply disappeared.

Chiyari turned to me, frowning. His eyes said *'And?'*, for deleting an inanimate object is nothing. Less than nothing. A simple act of storage.

"It's gone," I told him. "Deleted. Unrestorably. Nothing that you or anyone else could do would get it back."

The moment when he realized my intent was beautiful and terrible to see. His blue eyes widened, real *fear* in them for the first time, maybe, in his life.

He tried to disappear. To teleport safely far away, but my spiderweb code had done its work and he was trapped. None of his exit pings were reaching his server.

No one could hear him but me.

His face went ashen, deer-in-headlights still, and I watched him silently calculate the implications of his mortality.

"Please," he said, finally. "Please." His eyes held mine. There was fear in them, but also certainty. As though pleading must necessarily yield mercy.

Something twisted in me. I called to mind the memory of the photograph on his wall, the man's face juxtaposed with the splatter of his blood.

"You were going to kill Amy."

"Not, kill—not this," he said softly. "She would wake up afterwards. She would be alive."

"It doesn't matter," I said. And I realized I was drawing out the scene.

I could feel him running through his possible responses, through what to say that would not enrage me further. I could feel the tendrils of his mind, little whiplashes of code slamming against my barrier, against the laws of virtual physics below the level of visible reality.

Chiyari *was* brilliant—the defenses and workarounds he

had mustered on a whim were impressive, and might have worked if I had not been so well-prepared.

But I had known what I was up against. I was very well-prepared.

I found that, for the first time in more than two centuries of life, the possibility of my own death did not scare me; no more than the prospect of living on as a murderer myself, at any rate.

"I'll die with you," I proposed. "Then you won't be alone in it."

Chiyari smiled sadly, and behind his eyes I saw Martian sunsets and black razor-deer and wondering, wondering what would pass in this universe without him. "What difference would that make?" he asked.

"None," I admitted, and decided that I did not really want to die anyway. Not yet.

I wanted to see how my world handled it—the coming of true death to their world. Once it had been done, it could be done again. Immortality would no longer be a guarantee.

"Goodbye," I told Chiyari, and triggered the several-layers-deep code that would compel the silicon matrix to perform the ultimate travesty. To *delete* all instances of his code.

My bug would race back through his timeline, corrupting not only the man who stood before me but all previous 'save points' from which he could be restored. No grieving mother or criminal justice body would be able to undo it.

I'm ashamed to admit how much thought I put into how I wanted it to *look*.

Which would be more final, I'd wondered? Deleting everything within the boundaries that encompassed "Chiyari," to have his body vanish like his mind, like the program he had always been? Or to cause only the contents of his brain and mind to disappear, leaving a useless corpse to remind my people of what Bio death had been like?

I had decided, in the end, that the people of this world were too used to corpses. Half a dozen of them hung in Chiyari's studio, were re-created in living rooms, and no one seemed to find that unsettling anymore.

Absence would be worse. The thought of something *missing*. Here, nothing ever disappeared.

Chiyari did. My little code-bugs gnawed through his reality in a fraction of a second, and he was simply gone. The room stood empty before me as though no one else had ever been here.

For a moment the emptiness seemed vacuous and awful —part of me *had* liked him.

Then I straightened and stretched, savoring the warmth of programmed sunlight on my skin.

ON SPEAKING WITH THE STARS

Content warning: **This story involves giant insects and, toward the end, severe bodily injuries.**

This novelette has never before been seen in print.

Kit has never been afraid before. They've had *anxiety*—test anxiety, performance anxiety. And they thought they knew, from that, what fear was like.

But now adrenaline is like acid in their blood, threatening to drive them to—

What? Running will not stop the walls from shaking, rattling as though the shuttlecraft is about to fly apart. Hiding would be no escape from the solid surface that's hurtling up at them as they plunge into its gravity well.

Kit *knows*, in their mind, that there is nothing to be afraid of. The shuttle will slow itself and bring them smoothly to the ground. The chances of failure are so astronomically low as to be laughable. But their body doesn't know that.

The Reshaped worship the body and its animal instincts.

Why? This is awful.

They can, at least, pretend that the shaking is all coming from the ship. Maybe it is; maybe their limbs really aren't trembling nor their teeth chattering. It's hard to tell in the midst of this din.

Below, the planet grows. Kit tries to focus on that—on strangeness and newness and beauty. On potential. It's a tableau of jade oceans and continents, the land swirled pale on the dry plains and dark in the forests. There is something strangely compelling about the ribbon of atmosphere that glows on the curved horizon. Something compelling about the wildly curling shapes of peninsulas and archipelagos, the almost-random pattern of pale desert and dark jungle.

Kit tries to focus on the beauty. Tries *not* to think about the gravity well.

This titanic world is, by orders of magnitude, the largest thing they've ever seen. Its gravity well is the strongest physical force they've experienced. In Kit's mind's eye the space-time curve yawns before the shuttle, an irresistible incline that stops not at the planet's surface, but at its white-hot core. In Kit's mind's eye, the shuttle thrusters fail, and the surface intercepts them at an impossible speed—

Kit reaches for the override. Stops themself, trembling.

What's to become of an Eternal who does not trust mathematics to predict the future, who does not trust their ship to take them to a safe arrival?

I have faith in the equations.

At last the shaking does begin to cease, soothing quiet in its place as the curve of the horizon falls away. The tableau becomes a world; a waving substance Kit recognizes as *grass* ripples far below, and they marvel at convergent evolution.

They'll find almost exactly the same forms here, for the most part, as they would have on their ancestors' homeworld hundreds of lightyears away.

Kit cares little for the minutiae of biology, but feels something in their brain cataloguing it nonetheless, noting the microscopic differences between the structures of blades of grass from one world to the next. Catalog, catalog, catalog. You can never know too much.

They are no longer afraid. But now, more puzzling, Kit feels *sick*. Nausea rises.

A quick system scan shows many readings off, but no signs of physical damage. Nothing their training says cannot be stress-induced.

Kit breathes deeply, willing themself to calm. This is their final test. And they will pass it.

The shuttle levels and ribbon of atmosphere becomes a horizon.

The black ship descends from the jade sky, smooth and silent as a piece of the Void. This, Lily thinks, is what the end of the world looks like.

Strangely, she feels no fear. This was always certain. This outpost was only a temporary mercy; an attempt to give her purpose that no one had truly believed would work. It hadn't been a shock, then, when she failed to decipher the language of the Ants.

It *had* been a shock when her overs professed their intent to call in an Eternal. Her kind and theirs rarely trusted each other. But she had always known that *someone* would come to replace her. There were always going to be more people, more qualified and talented experts, coming in to take over her quiet world.

Lily chews her lip and tries not to think about returning. Tries not to think about what useless, interchangeable task they'll come up with for her next.

The black ship executes a smooth arc from vertical to horizontal until it's skirting across the plains. Copper-colored grass ripples beneath it, touched as though by breeze.

The oblong settles with a sound like a sigh, and Lily waits. When the door opens, it is a patch of brightness. The ship's carapace absorbs all light, seeming depthless; the interior is well-lit and white, from the glimpse that Lily sees. She expects an Eternal like the ones she's holoconferenced with; tall, thin, ephemeral things.

What steps out is thin and ephemeral, but it is—

Lily's mouth falls helplessly open.

It is a *child*.

The overs' transmissions make more sense, now. The way they'd stressed the Eternal's diet—that they would consume only their nutrient packets, had brought all they would need for the duration. That they had brought their own water filter, too, and that they were never to be left alone with the planet's native life.

As though their emissary would need looking after, as though—

Dear gods. They'd sent a child, not more than twelve years old.

And the child, as they take their first uncertain steps down the shuttle's gangplank, looks *afraid*.

Lily rushes out to meet them.

Why a child? It doesn't matter. *I will take good care of them.*

The Reshaped habitation sticks out like a sunspot. From the pale flatness of the plain, a geodesic dome rises. It's scarcely larger than Kit's shuttle. More than large enough for the single alien sentinel on this world. The Reshaped who has called for Kit's help.

Kit knows the Reshaped way. They'll send one sentinel, and one sentinel only, until the world's natives bid them leave or stay. Those who bid them stay will become partners in their exchange; if they are asked to leave, they'll slink away instead with a million covertly gathered genetic samples for their archives. Raw materials for new life, new generations of Reshaped.

Usually, that's all there is to it. But this is not a usual planet.

The figure that steps out of the dome's airlock as the shuttle descends is even stranger than Kit would have imagined.

In proportion, it is much like an Eternal—two arms, two legs, five fingers on the hand it raises in greeting. But as they draw nearer, Kit realizes that the thing is horribly mismatched—a jagged line down the middle of the face and body marks the border between two drastically different skin textures, and the whole form is asymmetrical. The half of the scalp with smooth skin is marked by drifting waves of hydrangea-blue hair, while the other half is scaled and hairless. A pale cat's eye regards her from one half of the face; a dark hawk's eye from the other.

They've never seen a Reshaped that looked like *this* in the vids.

Intimidating as the strangeness outside might be, Kit is *glad* to be free of the shuttle. They stumble out, swaying wildly under their own weight in the gravity. This world's rotation is different from that of her orbital creche, and her sense of vertigo still has not gone away.

The Reshaped strides forward, steady despite its odd design. Slows as it approaches Kit. Tentatively, offers Kit a hand to hold.

Kit is more glad of the assistance than they'd care to admit.

The Reshaped leads them—with unbearably obvious patience—toward the geodesic dome. Kit is looking forward to a familiarity of angles and line inside the habitation, but when the door opens, their body recoils in overwhelming reflex at what lays beyond.

Within the dome is a riot of plant life—a higher density, and more variety, than what's out here on the plains. The chaos of it is enough to send Kit's heart rate climbing again.

They are beginning to wonder if they will be perpetually on the edge of panic here; beginning to wonder how *low* the Reshaped have set their goals, that they can be happy amid such disorder.

Kit knows what a garden is; has seen the production facilities where necessary nutrients were produced and extracted. But theirs was a geometric beauty, a beauty of certainty, predictability, repetition. This is different. Vines strew as though wild, curling around the feet of the Reshaped woman who is—even stranger than Kit could have imagined.

The Reshaped is looking at them. Waiting. *Pitying.*

Kit leans away from the Reshaped, and vomits.

When their legs collapse under the weight of foreign gravity, the Reshaped picks them up and carries them inside.

The most unsettling thing about the child is their eyes. The Eternal overs Lily spoke to via holo had the same eyes—blank, crystalline spheres, tech in place of flesh, seeing things that Lily never could. The augmented senses were part of the reason her own overs called them.

But Lily's brain tells her that those eyes should be blind, and the way the child moves only makes them more unsettling. This Eternal is nothing like the Reshaped children Lily grew up with. They are too still, too calm, and too accepting. But even those, Lily realizes, are the wrong words. It's the *blankness* of Kit—the lack of emotion, once they were safely inside the walls of the little bungalow—that bothers Lily. An adult could be so disciplined, so emotionless, through years of long training; a child should not be.

How long do Eternals live? The answer is right there in their name; but Lily thought, thought she'd read, that their aging does not slow to a grinding halt until adulthood. Is this one stunted, for some reason? Are they special? A prodigy?

Lily is glad, secretly, that the child is still resting. Glad for the distraction of preparing dinner. A real, solid task for a surreal and disconnected day.

"What is this place for?" The voice is small, thin, flat.

Lily actually jumps. The knife she was using to chop root vegetables skitters across the cutting board.

"It's a...kitchen," she manages, turning to face the child.

The child, standing entirely too close, looks up at her with a frown of deep concentration.

"It's a food preparation area."

"Ah."

That question answered, the child moves on. They remind Lily of the exploration drones she runs across the plains, turning their attention mechanically from one problem to the next.

Kit makes a beeline for the pots and pans, and Lily wonders if she should stop them.

"You prepare your own food," the child murmurs as they examined the smooth metal surfaces. "From plants."

"Yes. And fungi."

Lily remembers the nutrient packs from the shuttle—liquids, as colorless as Kit's eyes. Enough to feed the child for months, according to the labeling.

"May I watch?" Kit seems, suddenly, just a little bit human as they turn from their inspection.

"I—of course."

And the child begins to look *happy* as they watch Lily chop herbs and roots from the garden.

Lily remembers the Eternals' instructions not to vary Kit's diet. They were afraid, Lily guessed, that she'd poison them. But the poor thing looks undernourished, and those nutrient packs are no kind of food.

"Could you eat like me," Lily asks, hesitantly, "if you had to?"

The crystalline eyes make it difficult to be sure, but the child seems to gaze into the middle distance. "It looks that way. Unless your people have changed in the last few years, we should have all the same digestive enzymes."

Lily stares, wondering, at this creature who couldn't stomach the garden but could tell which digestive enzymes they possess.

For a moment she forgets that Kit's crystalline eyes can see her, and are staring back.

The aromas that rise from the Reshaped's pan are confusing —tantalizing and repulsive, both at once. Kit's body seems at war with itself over what to do with this barrage of sensory information.

Kit fights for some more familiar mode of thinking. Focuses on visual information—on the Reshaped's mismatched hands.

"Why did they make you—like you are?"

The Reshaped stops. Her scaled hand ceases to toss the pan over the—fascination of fascinations, *open* flame. Her smooth hand, wielding the implement called *spatula*, goes still.

She says softly: "They didn't."

Kit waits.

"I was supposed to be—two people." The tossing of the pan resumes slowly. "We grew together in the womb. We weren't even supposed to be in the same womb—it was an accident of contaminated instruments."

The Reshaped quirks a smile that does not look at all happy. "Now 'we' are—'me.' I've never felt like two people, but that makes it easier to talk about. Even my brain—I'm told—the hemispheres don't match."

Kit absorbs this in silence. Tries to decide how to feel. The thought of a *mistake* in making a person is as fascinating and repulsive as the scent of the cooking food. It is not something their people do—their templates vary little, making an accident of that kind inconsequential even if it were to occur. Such accidents are unavoidable, they suppose, for people who tinker wildly with organic forms.

"Is that why you're here?" Kit asks.

The smooth-skinned half of the Reshaped face becomes redder, suffusing with blood. Kit remembers the same happening to them after giving an incorrect answer in a class, and instantly regrets the question.

"I am best-suited," the Reshaped says carefully, "for solo work. My talents and skills—do not mesh well into any team."

"Neither do mine," Kit offers, by way of reparation.

It's true, but not the same. Eternals are designed to work alone. Reshaped are not.

Kit can see the Reshaped's facial muscles working; can see

her struggling not to speak. At last she flips her pan-fried vegetables one last time and slides them into a bowl. The stuff looks, to Kit, like something you'd find dead in a neglected garden. But its scent is all caramelized sugars and flavors she cannot name—flavors very different from those of rot.

"Would you like a taste?" The Reshaped asks.

Kit hesitates, and it's with mixed horror and delight that they feel their head nodding.

The Reshaped holds out a pile of steaming vegetables on the end of a long metal stick. It takes Kit a moment to figure out what to do; at last, they lean forward and close their mouth around it.

The explosion of sensation makes their eyes water and their brain whirr. At first, it is wonderful—the nutrition is suboptimal, but the *experience* is something else.

And then the texture hits them. Dead things and slime.

Their body has rejected the gift before they can stop it, spewing bits and pieces across the Reshaped's counter.

Thankfully—and puzzlingly—the Reshaped is laughing.

Putting the Eternal to bed is a surreal experience.

Kit peruses everything like an uneasy animal in a new environment. Which, Lily supposes, they are. They were too depleted to scrutinize the bedroom before, and the sunset, she supposes, gives it an ominous shade.

The fact that they will not be an animal for long occurs to Lily, and she tries not to shudder.

It takes Lily a moment to understand why Kit is staring at the bed in confusion.

"You sleep on this...all night?"

"Yes. Like you did earlier."

"But I thought it was like a resting couch. You...why?"

Lily shakes her head, trying not to smile. "Because there isn't any other choice. You can't turn the gravity off here."

Kit looks profoundly distressed by this.

Finally the child climbs onto the bed. They pull the blankets over themself—and begin to toss and turn restlessly. Lily wonders if she should stay and watch—if the child might need the reassurance of her presence, or if they'd feel oppressed by it. If she were to ask, she gets the sense they'd be too proud to be honest.

At last the slender form beneath the blankets stills, their breaths slowing into sleep. Lily watches—finds herself relieved. This eldritch creature had survived its first night under her care.

In the dark and quiet of the bedroom, Lily wonders about the motives for preparing a *child* for such a journey. Among the Reshaped, there would have been injections of hormones and nanites and genes. Things to strengthen the heart and other muscles before subjecting them to the stress of new gravity, to prepare the immune system or an alien biochemistry. It was not an altogether error-free process, and certainly not a comfortable one. To neglect such a regimen before sending an agent into alien territory would be worse.

So why subject a child to a mission like this?

Lily has spoken by feed to Eternal adults—tall and slender creatures as only microgravity can produce, crystalline eyes like Kit's, who lectured her parentally about her guest-to-be's needs and safety.

They had not, apparently, felt the need to warn her about their agents' age. Had they assumed she'd know? Was this *normal* protocol for them? Or had they hidden it intentionally?

The child seems to be recovering from planetfall. Seems to have no ill effects from their one taste of real food. The caution with which they move even through the corridors of Lily's home make her think Kit is unlikely to wander off into danger, or do anything similarly stupid. They'll do their job —or fail—and return to her ship.

Can they do this job?

That's an angle Lily hadn't considered. Perhaps that's why the Eternals sent a child—at twelve they'd be at the peak of neuroplasticity, ready to learn a new language at the drop of a hat. They'd be adventurous, and *curious*.

Perhaps, then, Kit really will learn to speak to the Ants.

This world, Inanna, is a rare host of oxygen-carbon life. The discovery of photosynthesis here excited the Reshaped and the other children of humanity. Even the Eternals took a mild interest, briefly tearing one of their God-computers from its incomprehensible sums to orbit the world and examine it.

Lily's mission here is to discover if Inanna might surpass 'rare' and prove to be 'vanishingly so'—if its native life might prove sentient. True companions for Earth's children.

Thinking about the great, lumbering insects that carve complex patterns across the plains in Kit's bedroom makes Lily inexplicably uncomfortable. She glances one last time around the room to ensure the child has everything they need, then slips down the darkened corridor toward the garden.

She will sleep herself soon, but not yet.

The Ants present Lily with a unique problem. She'd been stationed on Inanna for the purpose of learning about it—a paradise prison for a misfit. The planet's thick and oxygen-rich atmosphere had allowed its eusocial insects to grow to an enormous size. Large enough to harbor a brain as big as a human's and at least as complex. When Lily began to suspect sentience, she'd known it was her duty to report it—almost guaranteeing, in the process, that she'd be replaced by a more capable team.

But her overs wanted *proof* of sentience on Inanna. And she couldn't find it.

How do you differentiate the intricate designs of a slime mold from those of a master architect? The efficiency of a dumb program from the work of a million minds? There were mathematical algorithms, but all of those were based on the assumption of individuality in behavior.

The Ants used tools; they farmed; they built cities, which displayed mindfulness toward specialized labor and complex social hierarchy. But they did not make *decisions*, as far as Lily could tell. Not as individuals.

They communicated through chemical signals. A language with potential for vast complexity, but devilishly difficult to interpret. How did one distinguish grammar or meaning from a chemical stew? The only thing Lily could positively do was correlate chemicals to the actions they prompted; and that was mechanistic behaviorism.

Most telling, the Ants reacted to Lily's presence no more than an animal might to a bird or a flower. They did not appear to be *curious*.

Yet their hives made startlingly complex decisions. The internal structures of abandoned hive caves contained what looked for all the world to be *art*, teardrops and spirals and waves of perfect symmetry, architecture with no purpose Lily could discern other than beauty. There were structures that spoke to her, not just of hierarchy, but of *reverence*.

And each year when the grasses ripened and turned golden, the same wave-and-spiral patterns would appear on the grass of Inanna's plains. Worker Ants would spend days trekking through the tall grasses, cutting stalks and collecting seeds in fractal patterns large enough to be seen from space. It could be natural behavior, some survival advantage to cutting different swaths of grain while leaving others to propagate each year.

But it just didn't look that way to Lily.

There was nothing in the Reshaped algorithms about making a judgement of sentience based solely on aesthetic designs. Still, the Reshaped had learned well to be cautious before treating other species as mere objects.

Were the Ants of Inanna a crop to be harvested, or partners to be respected and protected?

The Eternals, left to themselves, did not care. Lily was still a bit surprised that they had answered her overs' call. But they *did* like complex problems, and maybe this was one that even their crystalline eyes saw as challenging.

The Reshaped sought communion with the living world. Sentience not of Earth was a particularly rare gem. The overs would never forgive themselves if they missed it here. But they'd hit a brick wall, so far, in their attempts to talk to the Ants.

There was one solution they had already thought of, entertained and then discarded. It was just possible that a hominid could communicate with an Ant if the Ant's nervous systems were reproduced inside the hominid brain. If the right genes were expressed, the right neural wiring achieved, the hominid could experience what the Ants felt firsthand. Then they could *know*.

But the Ants' arthropoid nervous systems were a tangled and inscrutable mess. They didn't process information even close to the same way as a hominid brain. And the Reshaped overs wouldn't put an arthropoid nervous system into a one of their own until they knew what it *did*. Mistakes of the sort that could create a damned offspring were to be avoided at all costs.

Lily looks down at her own mismatched hands.

Mistakes.

She had been lucky, given the circumstances. Her two halves fused and read each others' signals, working together to compensate for duplication. Where she could have had two heads, a single brain had formed; where organs could have been unevenly duplicated, placing fatal stress on the system, she was whole.

The cooperation of her two halves had been so seamless that no one had even noticed she was not developing as planned until her fourth month in her creche's womb.

They could have terminated her. If she had lacked limbs or a healthy brain, they would have. But the fusion of her halves seemed to be producing something new; something unplanned and imperfect, but functional and just possibly exciting. The newness of her had been an asset, had almost, for a time, spawned talk of trying to do this sort of thing on purpose.

The Reshaped, after all, adore new things.

Her overs had watched with slow-growing disappointment as she failed, one by one, to excel at crucial skills. Her two halves had different bone structures; she would work twice as hard to attain any sort of physical grace or skill, would never be innately gifted in that realm. The two halves of her brain sometimes produced unique attitudes or insights as a result of their interplay, but failed to perform any kind of thought as quickly as her peers.

Her psyche, ultimately, was what shattered it. From infancy it had been impossible *not* to notice that she was different. And Reshaped adults did not believe in lying. Her frighteningly mismatched appearance had been eschewed by other creche children from the time they were old enough to talk. She'd been told, around the time she learned to ask, that she was different. Around the time she learned to read, in the gentlest possible terms, that she was a mistake.

Mistakes like her didn't happen, so no one knew how to

handle them. If something went wrong, usually, it was so bad that the fetus had to be destroyed.

So she had muddled through her studies and apprenticeships; always just good enough, never excellent. Always good enough to receive kindness; always slow enough to suspect that whatever kindness she received was out of pity.

This assignment had been given out of pity. A planet, maybe dangerous, that no one knew what to do with. Low enough priority to be non-urgent; a big enough game that she couldn't possibly screw it up beyond repair.

Throw in the chimera, and see what she can do with it.

But she couldn't solve it; could not make the least progress for her people. The natives she'd been sent to speak with paid her less attention than a blade of grass. Their brains and genes were as opaque to her as Kit's inscrutable eyes.

The only thing she *does* seem to be good at is meditating. And that has taken her a long way. Lily sits amid the plants of her garden, and breathes her terror out into the earth.

Watching the Reshaped is fascinating.

The name Kit's overs chose for them seems to be working; the Reshaped is engaging in classic parental behaviors. As they lie down and pretend to sleep, Kit slows their breath and waits to see how long the Reshaped will stand watching them. Tries to let their body rest; knows they need it.

But there is so much to learn here.

After the Reshaped has finally left, they creep from the flat little bed and into the corridor. Into the sweeping breeze pungent with strange plant scents.

And know immediately that something is wrong.

The air is so thick as to be stifling; the scents are not

Earth scents, not food scents. The geodesic dome has developed a breach; a big one, if Kit's senses are any guide.

They scamper through the corridor to find the Reshaped, and to help her.

The corridor opens onto the Reshaped garden. The mad tangle of vegetation is nothing like the gardens of home. Kit stubs their toe on an errant tree root. Drops into a crouch, waiting for the pain to pass. Stares, fascinated at the damage; red blood wells up from beneath torn skin.

And then Kit looks up.

The Reshaped's dome has opened like a flower. Intentionally, Kit now understands. And above them are—

Stars. Stars like nothing they have ever seen.

Stars are almost all the landscape Kit knows. They are the landmarks by which Eternals navigate. The *only* landmarks in the Void. Kit has seen them through the viewports of their creche since birth. They've been Kit's destination since they were old enough to know what they were meant for.

But these stars are *different*. They are set, not in the hard black emptiness of Void, but in the soft blue-black velvet of an atmosphere. Inanna's gases overlay them like a veil, softening and scattering their light. These stars are sheathed in mystic auras like some ancient flame. They twinkle. The pictures they paint are no mere landmarks; they are majesty.

Kit's stars are bright, hard objects; clean, cold facts. These are soft wraiths, mystery-shrouded spectres. They cycle through every spectral band and finds the tapestry equally beautiful in each.

Kit realizes that they have plunked themself down on the enclosure floor, all concern forgotten, when they hear a twig snap some meters away. An animal sense, older than time, fills them with that awful *fear* again. They freeze and stare into the darkness. Think, after an embarrassingly long pause, to switch to infrared.

The shape of Lily blazes into being in the darkness, crossed in places by the cold black limbs of trees. And the Reshaped is doing something *odd*.

She is standing beneath the stars, arms upraised, and she is speaking. Her lips move and her breath moves with them, though Kit can hear no sound. She is talking, quite clearly, to the stars.

To her overs?

No. Kit cycles through spectrums and sure enough; even looking right at Lily, this enclosure is radio-dark the way Kit's ship never was. There is no signal. Lily is not transmitting anything that anyone could pick up.

Kit creeps closer—and jumps as their own foot snaps a twig. The Reshaped turns to stare in their direction, startled.

"What are you doing?" Kit asks innocently to cover their eavesdropping. Their voice sounds, to their own ears, like an invader in the silence.

"I was—looking at the stars." Something almost like shame creeps into Lily's voice.

Kit accepts this for the moment. Moves forward to stand beside Lily in the clearing, letting starlight fall on them for the Reshaped's animal eyes.

"Why?" Kit asks.

"Because—it just feels like you should. Doesn't it?"

Kit must admit that it does. This is a thing to be explored—the instructions must be ancient, ancestral, to be written in both their bones. Kit looks up, feeling anxious then. They want to do something and they can't explain why. That is *rare*. No one ever talked about this in their classes.

"Isn't it a quarantine violation," Kit asks finally, "to open your dome like this?"

In the infrared, Lily's shoulders heave. "We'll do worse before we leave this place."

Kit suppresses alarm; betrays nothing. In their haste for a change of subject, says: "You were *talking* to the sky."

"Yes." Something in Lily's voice is defensive. "What's wrong with that?"

"They can't hear you."

Lily stands from her half-crouch, looking up again. "I know."

Kit waits for further explanation. It occurs to them that the Reshaped is stopping because she feels the need to *put Kit back to bed*, and that rankles something in them.

"Why do it, then? And why open the dome?"

"Our ancestors looked up at the stars," Lily says, as though that explains everything. "They wanted to talk to them. If they hadn't, we wouldn't be here."

Kit is stunned to realize that that's *true*. Feels, somehow, as though they're on the defensive now: "They needed somewhere to expand after they had used up Earth."

Lily shakes her head, as though Kit were an incorrigible child.

That is the wrong response.

"I know that you Reshaped are atavists," Kit says, a little more harshly than they need to. "But what good can these old rituals do you? What are they worth?"

Lily goes still and quiet. She's beside Kit now, and reaching for their hand. Kit takes it, glad to play a role if it means an end to this ridiculousness. To their surprise, Lily pulls her not toward the house, but out into the center of the clearing.

"Try it," she says.

Kit obeys reflexively. Larger people have always been their overs, and in this darkness the things that mark Lily as Reshaped are hidden. They crane their neck to look up, and find that they cannot look away.

Something about this feels odd. Dangerous.

What if they try these animal things, things of biochemistry and flesh, and discover that they *like* them?

It won't matter. After Graduation, it won't matter.

They find themself scanning the sky for moving stars. For neighbors, comings, goings. But the sky above Inanna is as empty as its continents. The only certain sentience on this world is found here in this garden.

Kit feels suddenly, plungingly, alone.

"Who do you think is up there?" Lily asks.

Kit reaches for an answer. "Other planets." Tries to imagine other worlds as strange and thick with scents as Inanna; worlds with stars of other spectra, with vegetation varying in form.

"Why?" asks Lily.

"Because *stars have planets.*" Kit doesn't know what else to say.

They hear the brush of hair as Lily shakes her head. "No. Why are there planets? Why are there stars?"

"That's what we're trying to find out," Kit says, their voice low and cold.

Lily goes still and silent. Startled.

"You didn't know that, did you? If you studied us with half the fervor you use to study these insects—with half the attention you use in cooking—you would have known. What do you think we need big brains for, or long lives?" Kit feels patience seeping into her bones, the stars lulling them to calm. "Questions of creation cannot be answered by animal brains. They're simply not built for it. They're built only to survive."

Kit knows they've just insulted Lily—and her entire society—in the vilest possible way. They've invalidated their philosophy, said that their approach is useless. Kit wonders if the Reshaped will even take that as an insult, her priorities being so evidently *different.*

"That's why we respect you," Lily says softly.

Kit freezes. She didn't understand the insult. Or—

"You do what we cannot imagine," Lily continues. "You shed your skins. You do the higher maths. I knew that. I just thought that maybe—you could hear them too."

Kit realizes they are still staring at the stars. They feel their blood beginning to race—why?

"...hear what?" Kit manages.

Is the Reshaped mad? Kit wonders. Or are they deprived of some mysterious sense as Lily is deprived of infrared vision?

"The—presence—" Lily manages. "It feels as though there's something out there, doesn't it? *Someone.*"

Kit resists the urge to turn and stare at the Reshaped. Starts cycling through spectrums instead, as though something in the sky might explain the statement.

"Our ancestors used to call them gods. And maybe—maybe they weren't entirely wrong. We've proven that they correlate better to the hearer's psychology than to any objective theology. But maybe that's just bias in interpreting the perception of something real."

"You're theists," Kit says, dismayed.

"No more than you are. Not by much, at any rate."

Kit stands up. Feels anger, disappointment. Things they've rarely had cause to feel before. There was promise here. The promise of new things. But their overs were right; the Reshaped's pursuit is nonsense, self-defeating.

"It's good for us," Lily tries, "to talk to ourselves. To talk to our perceptions of the Universe."

"It's the worst kind of mistake. Mistaking yourselves for gods."

"We don't—"

"It's the kind of mistake that gets people killed." Kit is stomping toward the compound, stories of holy wars unspooling in their head. It wasn't just the wars, of course—it was the miscalculations, the over-optimisms, the failure to take proper precautions under the assumption of a caring Universe.

It was everything that almost killed their species in its infancy.

It's the fact that if any of their people ever believed Lily right, they'd stop searching for the real answers. The right ones.

An uneasiness pierces the usual euphoria as Lily rises.

She feels the breezes from the open roof; tastes her Earth and Inanna both on the wind. But her body remembers something troubling.

Remembers Kit.

Lily sits up, groaning. She should never have introduced the Eternal to anything controversial; should never have deviated from the overs' care plan for the child. She had been prepared, as the oblong descended, to confine her conversation to the polite. To avoid diplomatic incidents.

But she had been expecting an adult. A stiff and distant creature who would keep to their own quarters, who would guard the boundary of offense as vigilantly as she. Not a child who would inspire the teacher in her; not a curious seeker who would come creeping after her in the dark.

She passes the bedroom she'd set up for her guest. Finds the door open, the bed unmade, empty. Suppresses alarm; tries to imagine the child-thing doing something stupid.

Kit is sitting on the kitchen counter, silently sucking her nutrition mix from a pouch.

"Good morning." Lily hears the chill in her own voice; wonders if she'll hold a grudge against the child-thing.

"Morning." Kit's voice is almost repentant. Lily glances up at its crystalline eyes, and softens. Remembers arguing with her own creche teacher at a similar age.

"What do you want to do today?" she asks the child, gently. A coded way to ask if she needs more time to recover from planetfall.

"I want to see the Ants," Kit says immediately, sucking on her nutrient pouch. "As soon as possible."

They're in a hurry to be rid of me.

"Alright," Lily grants. "After breakfast."

In the hours after sunrise, the Ants begin to stream from their mountain caves.

Lily ferries Kit to within a half-kilometer of the cave, her all-terrain vehicle heaving and bumping over the almost entirely untraveled plains. Kit watches through magnifying lenses as huge, black forms clamber from an opening in the mountainside in comically impossible numbers.

"Yesterday," Lily says, "they ran a herd of wildebeest off of a cliff. They brought many of the carcasses back, but there's more work to do. They stop at night—I think their metabolisms suffer from the cold."

Kit watches the parade of monsters vanishing into the tall grass without comment. Lily brings them in closer.

Though the Ants have never shown any interest in her, Lily still treats them as she would a perceptive—and potentially dangerous—creature. She gives the line a warning honk of the ATV's horn as she draws near. The worst thing you can do is *surprise* a wild animal. When they don't respond, she turns the car to parallel the lumbering workers, following the line back to the cave entrance.

"Put this on." She hands Kit a spray bottle, which the child stares at dumbly.

"It's a pheromone. A safety measure. It makes you smell like one of them."

Kit narrows their eyes. "What happens if you go in without it?"

Lily shrugs. "Nothing. But still. Safety measure."

The child relents and sprays themself, making a face as they do so.

The workers are a little smaller than Lily's vehicle. Curled up, she could fit into one of them three times—one for each body segment. The sense-hairs on their legs stick out like thorns, and their heads look like pressure helmets with vicious vicegrips attached to the front.

"Interesting," Kit comments, leaning over Lily to get a closer look. Again, the child's lack of emotion disturbs her.

No fear. Disgust at the sensation of the spray, but no fear of death.

Lily imagines the child's broad-spectrum eyes analyzing, cataloguing, seeing everything there is to see about these creatures.

The Ants turn their heads in unison to follow the van as it grows nearer to the cave entrance. It is this that has Lily's overs convinced that, for all their engineering marvels, these creatures can't be sentient.

Each time she approaches, they regard her with this clockwork uniformity; every time they turn away, content, apparently, at the smell of her. The workers display no further curiosity; do not deviate from their tasks to investigate the alien arrival.

"Our best bet to talk to them," Lily tells Kit, "is to go inside."

The soldier Ants are worse than the workers. Their jaws are more sawblades than vices, their carapaces like tanks. Ten Lilies could fit inside a soldier, she has estimated. She cannot repress the urge to herd Kit behind her as she climbs out of the ATV, as though this were some protection.

Perhaps more significantly, Kit lets her do it.

She knows that the operation is safe, or she wouldn't have brought the Eternal child. She's done it dozens of times before—a dozen missions wandering the honeycombed halls of this hive, mapping them, seeing strange and terrible wonders. Wonders like something from Earth—from a beehive, or the brilliant engineering of a slime mold.

Or wonders like city streets, like architecture, like temples?

When the soldiers are past, Kit loses their momentary hesitation. They slip around Lily and take the lead through the passage which darkens with alarming speed. Lily withdraws a globe from her pocket and lights it up.

In the eerie yellow-green shadows that radiate from the globe, Kit turns to her. It occurs to Lily to wonder if those blank eyes could see before she lit up the sphere—to wonder *what* they can see in the dark.

The child's expression is inscrutable.

They follow the trail past dark cells which are, as far as Lily can tell, abandoned. Past workers who clatter blindly past the strangers with the glowing orb, as though they were not there.

At a junction, two workers stand delicately tapping each other with antennae. Mandible-clicks without form or pattern pass between them.

Kit creeps close—so close that Lily fights the urge to reach out and grab them. But the Ants confer only a moment longer before skittering apart, following different branches of the forking passage.

Kit says something so softly that Lily can't make it out. She walks to hover, protectively, over them.

"What?" she whispers.

"I said," Kit snaps, "it's as I thought." Kit sounds—is that *fear* in their voice?

"Insects on Earth—ones like this—communicated primarily through scent. There may be a sonic component to their language, but if so it's only a modifier, like body language."

Lily's heart soared to hear the Eternal repeat her conclusion. "Then you think they do *have* a language?"

"They have a language," Kit says with perfect calm. "There's too much—" they frown—frustrated, Lily realises, by a lack of words to communicate with her. "The math," they say, slowly, almost patronizingly, "is wrong. None of this would work without a language-forming mind."

"What makes you—"

"The angles just don't fit together right!"

Kit says it so loudly that Lily reflexively gathers them close, looking over her shoulder for monsters. The Ants have never reacted to sound before, but old instincts die hard—and sometimes, Lily knows, that's for the best.

"Let's go," she whispers.

Kit complies and Lily shepherds them toward the exit, lighting their way with her gold-green sphere.

The words sit on Kit's tongue like nausea, all the way back to Lily's dome. Like the acid-fear of space-sickness. But much worse.

They let them fall, finally, when they are standing in Lily's kitchen. A comparatively white, angular space. Like home.

"You're going to have to Reshape me."

Lily actually drops the roots she was carrying in from the garden. Turns to stare at Kit. There's something endearing about that stare, about those huge, mismatched animal eyes.

"I need to be able to smell what the Ants can smell," Kit begins, gritting their teeth. "You couldn't do it—we'll need my brain's algorithms, and its processing power."

Lily has gone to one knee on the ground and is gathering up the roots, slowly.

"I felt..." Kit struggles to articulate. Names of fractal patterns and mesh-webs will do her no good here. "I felt something *big*." They remember the strange fluttering in their stomach as they watched the way the Ants moved—as they imagine the spread of their cave system through the mountains, carved with painstaking care.

"I felt something *conscious*. Something alive. Something your people," they rush to remind Lily, "would want to know about."

"How's that? Are you psychic?"

Kit hears the crossness in Lily's voice, and understands it.

"I'm mathematical. And perceptive. That's why your overs sent for me. We can do things that you can't, with our augments. But we can't—engage—as you do."

"You mean," Lily says softly, "that you haven't studied the Reshaping of organic bodies."

Kit shrugs. "It has not seemed worthwhile to us."

"Is that why they sent you?" Lily asks suddenly.

Kit stares. Bites their tongue.

"A child. That's why they sent a child, isn't it? They knew you'd need an organic body, and one that was easy to modify."

"That's not the only reason," Kit blurts out. Lily's words feel too much like an accusation—too much like a refusal—to stay silent.

Lily waits.

"I asked for a hard test. For my final exam. If I pass," Kit hesitates. Are they baring too much to this near-stranger, not even one of their own people? "If I pass, if I solve the problem—I get to Graduate."

"I'm in the bottom cohort, among my creche," Kit hears their voice go quiet as they say it, hates their own weakness in the face of the truth. "Not slated to Graduate. Not as it stands right now. So my overs thought they could—" they almost say *risk me*, but stop themselves in time.

"They thought they could test me, to see what I can do when faced with a unique challenge. If I pass, I get a big brain. If not, *creche duty*." Kit hears the contempt dripping from their own voice. Wonders if Lily knows that, among the Eternals, creche-keepers are the only ones to be denied the higher geometries, the only ones to grow old and die.

Lily is staring at them with something like horror on her face. "You...Graduate," she says the word carefully, knowing what it means, "so early?"

That is the Reshaped's concern?

"Sooner is better," Kit explains. "Organic bodies can die. Each passing year is a chance of data loss."

Lily looks away, as though she cannot bear to meet Kit's eyes. Puts the basket of roots on the kitchen counter, pretends to be busy with them.

"So if I don't...change you," Lily hesitates, "they'll deny you your Graduation?"

"Yes." It's simpler to say that than to explain the alternatives.

"And you...*want* to graduate?"

"More than anything."

Lily looks up, surprised at the emotion in Kit's voice.

Their eyes meet for an interminable moment. Kit can see that this goes against Lily's conscience. Can feel, also, the pitiful pleading in their own eyes.

You should not need this. Your logic should be enough to convince.

Lily is an animal, Kit's defenses kick in. *Logic doesn't work on animals.*

The moment stretches. Long, long. What if Lily refuses?

"I'll do it," the Reshaped says, very softly.

Relief floods Kit. Then terror. They won't be like the rest of their people, after this. It may go wrong. Even if it goes right, they may fail.

Kit shakes their head. They must not fail. They cannot afford to.

Not at so high a price.

Nothing in Eternal teachings technically *forbid* Reshaping. The flesh is a tool—an incubation chamber—to be shed as soon as possible. It is not sacred, and so there was no taboo around its alteration.

But there is fear. Fear of damage. Fear of mistakes.

In their incubation years, Eternals are vulnerable like they never will be again. Changes to the organic flesh could warp a mind while the patterns necessary for sentience are being laid down. The worst-case scenario, neurological destruction—what worse crime could there be, than to destroy a mind?

To take *alien* flesh into their own—the flesh of a mere animal, not yet out of its species' Stone Age—

Kit actually shudders.

But this is the only way.

And beneath their terror, there's a tiny grain of perverse pride.

The danger makes this a *hard* test. The hardest, maybe, of their generation. If they do this thing and succeed, they will be a legend. They will be able to go wherever, to *know* and *think* anything...

Their stomach turns a little as they think of the second part of their success.

Translating the language of the Ants will be one triumph. Maybe an invaluable one. Though the views of organic life forms are generally considered negligible by the overs, as their brains have such limited capacities—there may be new algorithms here. New data.

And that's not all.

Kit imagines they can feel the rare earth metals in this planet's crust, singing beneath their feet. And that scares them, now, more than the Reshaping.

Lily breathes deeply as she preps the syringe. This is not what she expected. To care for the child, yes. To ensure that the Kit remained in perfect health. To send them back to their mysterious overs, intact and unharmed. Or risk repercussions.

How do Eternals respond if you harm one of their own? Lily doesn't know. She can't remember ever hearing of such a thing. There is no overlap between the territory of the Reshaped and the Eternals; the Eternal adults slide between the stars, black and silent and impossibly aloof. The Reshaped live in forest groves and under oceans, traveling through the black of space only by necessity.

Lily has never heard of anyone injuring an Eternal. Or having the opportunity.

But now the child lays before her on an exam table, crystalline eyes staring up at the ceiling. They say they know what they're doing. They say it matter-of-factly, as though their body were a machine and not the very fabric of their being.

To Kit, Lily supposes, that is true. To them, their

augments, the digital recorders of their organic thoughts, are what really matters. These are all that will survive their "Graduation."

"I need to be able to smell what they smell," Kit said. "If I'm right, their words are all around us."

Lily had known to investigate for pheromones. She had known that there were certain macro-patterns to their movements corresponding to wind patterns and to chemical traces left on blades of grass.

She had dared to hope that this might reach the level of a spoken language—that there might be sufficient variation to express thoughts, feelings, ideas. And Kit, and Eternal, had reached the same hypothesis on their own. There was a thrill in that.

But the next step makes Lily question everything. Is this problem worth solving, at such a high cost?

The Reshaped had sequenced the Ants' genomes in the first days after the remote probes discovered them in their loving swoops over Inanna. Long before Lily had been assigned here, their chemical data had been sent to some smarter, sleeker scientists in some warm and welcoming Reshaped colony, in a forest or beneath a sea. Nothing had looked, obviously, like language.

"But it wouldn't." Kit said, as Lily talked it over with them. "Do the genes for our eardrums specify that we speak? No. Pattern and meaning would be deciphered in the brain. Your people haven't figured out how to extract neural growth patterns from DNA, yet. The targeting mechanisms are too complicated for you."

"My people…"

"Mine have." Kit had looked at her with milky, owl-like eyes. "If you reverse-engineer the human genome with the higher maths, you can extrapolate the chemical signals that underlie the competitive wiring of the human brain."

Lily understood about half of that.

"I," Kit said, "can do the same for the Ants. And replicate them. In here." They tapped their head, the skull beneath pearl-white hair and the translucent sheath of skin. "But my olfactory bulbs need to have the receptors to hook the neural apparatus up to. That's where you come in."

And so Kit now lay on the table, waiting for Lily to inject them with the virus that would rewrite their senses, and part of their nervous system.

Lily threads the catheter carefully into the vein of Kit's arm.

"The odds of rejection," she explains, trying to sound as calm as Kit seems, "are low. But do let me know if you begin to feel anything strange. You shouldn't feel anything at all. Not yet."

And it occurs to Lily, as she compresses the plunger to push the solution into Kit's arm, that Kit does not know what they're doing.

They know the risks. Lily has no doubt of that. But do they know what it will *mean* if they succeed?

If Kit is right and there is meaning here—then the Ants represent a whole new way of being conscious. A way fundamentally different from the mammalian, individualistic paradigm that is all humanity has ever known.

Kit would be discovering a whole new kind of *people*.

In the Eternal view, access to the language would be access to just another data set. The presence or absence of the scent receptors was, to them, a binary 'yes' or 'no.' Do you have tools to perceive these chemicals, or don't you? Do you have the tools to know what data they represent, or don't you? All the data was going to the same place eventually—to the silent silicon brains between the stars. To the monoliths of thought—not experience.

The Reshaped would have other ideas.

To the Reshaped, the body *was* the self. What the Eternals regarded as a necessary evil they had not yet figured out how to replace, the Reshaped regarded as the purpose of life itself. The network of bone and nerve and muscle, the chemical interplay between them; cells could produce infinite variations of experience that silicon couldn't.

To the Eternals, experience was a means to the end of obtaining data. To the Reshaped, it was the other way around.

Lily pictures her planet swarmed by Reshaped. Good, competent translators chosen or made for this work. Her planet would become a new frontier—no longer a place of exile or solace for a mistake like herself, a woman of no conscious design. It would become the place where a new branch of humanity grew, feeding on everything the Ants could offer, starving and explosive in their curiosity after millennia of beating feebly at the boundaries of the range of human experience.

The people with the modification Lily is testing on Kit will smell differently, hear and see differently, *think* differently. They will be alien.

If it works. Lily watches Kit's breath come fast and ragged.

"Are you alright?" Lily asks, glancing at her monitor. The Eternal's heart rate is climbing.

"Just—nervous."

"Just a few more minutes," Lily promises, "until we're done."

"That," Kit says, "is what I'm scared of."

Kit sleeps as though dead. The changes to their brain give them strange and vivid dreams—nightmares of insectoid creatures, dragging them to a horrible fate.

The insects become their overs. Leering, terrifying things. Threatening a brief and painful existence. Kit finds themself assuming that the Ants are going to eat them. But then—

The Ants begin to speak.

There are no words for the things they say. No words—only something like feelings. And the things they say are rich, deep, *welcoming*. The Ants in Kit's dream accept them as the Eternals never did.

You are Hive. You are Home.

Kit knows, somewhere in their mind, that it is a dream.

But it is a *beautiful* dream.

When Kit awakens, the grassland has come alive with scent. It glows, and it sings.

Kit's brain reaches for other metaphors for the...color map? Symphony?

The algorithms in their implants hum beyond the speed of conscious thought, and sensations take on emotional depths and nuances that she cannot describe.

You are Hive. You are Home.

That which appears empty and silent is not. The fields around Lily's dome are like a canvas, painted anew each season for tens of thousands of years.

Kit basks in the flow of information they do not yet know how to interpret. The way it comes to them—as sensation—is unsettling.

What if I try these animal things, and like them? What will it be like to give them up?

But at the end of it all will be a gold mine of new facts. That is worth any price.

Deep inside their skull, Kit's implant is learning. Tomorrow it will understand.

For tonight Kit will lie with Lily in the garden, being held and fed sweet drinks that comfort their soft, animal body. Tonight they will listen to the grasslands, and watch Lily talk to the stars.

This time, it's Lily who follows Kit into the cave.

The giant, eldritch things moving unnaturally around her are as terrifying as ever. More so today, now that Kit has taught her how to initiate contact. Real contact. How to be accepted as one of their own.

She's armed, of course. But what is a plasma pistol to a ton of armored insect with jaws like a harvester's blades? She doubts the thing has a heart to stop, or that its body would stop coming if she took out its brain.

The Ants ignore them. As though they were part of the scenery, blades of grass.

They are stopped, briefly, by a soldier. Its chitinous blade dips dangerously close to Kit's shoulder, and Lily has her pistol armed, until—

Until Kit does *something*—lowers their face to a soldier's shell and stays there for a long, unearthly moment.

After that moment the soldier returns to its routine patrol, as though Kit were just another worker.

"To talk to them," Kit told Lily, while they recovered in her arms this morning, "we must first be recognized as kin. They'd no more talk to us than you would to a stone. There are ways of indicating—of pretending—our membership in their tribe. Ways to add ourselves to the gene pool that they recognize."

"Are they...smart?" Lily asked.

Kit thought for a moment. Nodded. "Yes. They think and feel very deeply."

And Lily's heart began to race. Already she was hungering, craving the new vistas Kit must be feeling. But Kit told her she must wait.

"You would be out of commission—for days—if your brain did what mine has. And it might not work on you. Better that we start them learning about us now."

So Lily did as Kit instructed—took samples of her own DNA, one from each side of her body. Amplified and purified until the source code to make Lily—both halves of her—was suspended thickly in pure water.

"A new Queen is hatching." Kit had sniffed the air cryptically. "Probably today. Go to her, and offer yourself. Offer what you took from them. DNA."

Now, Kit leads her through the Ant tunnels with a strange confidence. Moves as though following a drumbeat Lily can't hear.

It is *dark*. Kit warned her about that. The Ants would have no need for light to shed on the chemical roadmaps of their homes. So Lily brought light—her sphere that glows warm and penetrating, and a high-beam of cold white for sounding out distant objects.

She steps over strange obstacles as they venture deeper. Rotting logs that must have been dragged in from a distant forest and inadvertently dropped; smooth, jointed *limbs* that must once have belonged to the dead or injured members of the colony. Lily follows, fitting into the spaces between the busy workers and the walls.

The hive grows warmer. The walls, this far in, are no longer natural. They are *carved*. Their texture is the gouge-marks of diamond-hard mandibles, softened only slightly by the weathering of untold centuries. Foreign smells permeate the air. Lily wonders if the pheromones are so dense here that even she can taste them, or if the scents are simple byproducts of decay.

Kit stops, so suddenly that Lily runs into their outstretched arm. A child's arm—for a moment, she is struck by the absurdity of the scene.

And then she hears it. A clacking. The clacking of a thousand mandibles, not in synchrony, but in something like it. Rhythm. Then, the drumming of ten thousand legs. The ground begins to shake.

Kit takes Lily through an opening, and into total darkness.

The place is far too big for the light of Lily's sphere. The light glances off curved thoraxes, antennae waving ghostly in the dark. The Ants are dense here, and still. Lily cannot see the edge of the crowd.

She hesitates. Pauses. Different origin of life be damned, she can sense the sacred here. It is the sense of thousands gathered, waiting.

How will the Ants react to a high-beam flashlight in a dark and sacred space?

She turns it on and sweeps it over the assembled sea of chitinous backs. Across Kit's face, which wears something like ecstasy.

The silence! The frustrating silence! What Lily would not give to know what Kit, what the Ants, are experiencing.

As it reaches the center of the chamber, her beam sweeps across a—*thing*. A horrible, writhing organic mass like a maggot the size of Lily's dome. Her stomach turns and she shrinks back involuntarily.

"Come," Kit urges, seizing Lily's hand with fingers too gentle to resist. She threads them through the crowd—

ducking under legs, scooting perilously between massive, swaying abdomens; past enormous, unseeing eyes.

The Ants seem not to notice them, even as they approach the Holy of Holies.

The writhing mass, Lily understands now, is an enormous pupa. The fleshy covering is not the essential part here; through an opening at the front, a wet and shining Queen is being born to adulthood. She will be a new mother, a mother to ten thousand.

Meters from the platform, Lily stops and finds that she cannot go further.

Even to her, the emerging face of the Queen is beautiful.

There's a beauty in its sleekly swooping lines, in the exotic angles of its eyes. Its mandibles resemble ceremonial swords more than cleavers, sharp in the way of a blade that has never been used. And there is something beautiful about the act of its emergence—this is alien, no squalling babe, but even Lily's most primitive mind cannot miss the potential in the legs unfurling from the pupa.

Kit does not try to pull her further.

The Queen stands on trembling legs—a monarch and a newborn lamb at once. And something new and vast swoops in the space above her, creating air currents that even Lily feels.

She swings her flashlight to see wings. Wet, and glittering, razor-thin stained glass.

"Now," Kit's whisper comes in her ear, amplified by the earlinks they're wearing in case of separation.

One of the servants around the Queen is *extruding* something. Lily tries not to retch at the act of reverse eating—reminds herself that stomachs are the standard storage unit, the pottery of this people.

The *something* is thick and, Lily has no doubt, sweet. The nectar of ten million flowers, or some much stranger harvest.

It somehow holds the surface tension of a droplet, though it is large enough that Kit could swim inside.

"*Now.*" Kit shoves her forward with small arms.

Lily walks forward, trembling. Extends her arms over the enormous droplet. Feels like an uninvited participant in this alien sacrament.

At the droplet's other end, the Queen has already begun to drink.

Lily opens her vial of clear water and DNA. The liquid splashes onto the larger droplet, merges with it, disappears.

A gift for a gift. The genetic wealth of humanity for the genetic wealth of this new world.

A stillness, a silence falls.

She watches the droplet shrink, shaking, and thinks now she understands the old Earth expression "fear of God." This is fear, yes, of a thing who could cleave her in two with a second thought. But a thing, also, of incomprehensible beauty.

The shrinking stops. The Queen's antennae quiver.

And then all hell breaks loose.

***

Afterwards, it takes Lily a long time to piece together what has happened.

The assembled insects seemed to move as one. Where or *why* they were moving, Lily could not know. There was no room for directional movement in this packed amphitheatre. There was only a sudden chaos.

It was their small size that saved them—Lily remembers, through a haze of adrenaline-panic, Kit's small hand firmly dragging her between the agitated bodies. Remembers being buffeted by milling legs, dodging bobbing abdomens. At least once, a pair of mandibles *started* to close on her arm, but her arm was so slender that they could not close fast enough to catch her.

The ground shook, the chamber shook, the *mountain* shook, dislodging fragments of rock from the ceiling.

Too many fragments.

That must be how she came to be where she is now, panting in the dark. She is in a small space—a pocket created in the rockfall that separated her from the Ants.

She is alone.

"Kit?" she whispers, as though the Ants might hear her. Maybe they would, now. Maybe they would care now. What had gone so horribly wrong?

There is a faint, hissing static in her ear. That is very bad.

"Kit...can you…"

She tries to imagine something which would break the earlink without breaking the head it was attached to. Tries to imagine a way for the tiny, form-fitted device to fall off and be crushed underfoot, without crushing—

"Lily?" Is it the earlink or Kit's voice that sounds wrong? "Lily I'm...here."

Lily prays that it is fear, not pain, in the child's voice.

"Where is 'here?'" Lily asks, as though she had any point of reference from which to navigate.

"Near...an entrance. I can see light. I think...the same tunnel as you, but closer to the entrance, maybe."

Lily had dropped both the lights before she lost hold of Kit's hand. Now she feels, blindly, at the rough contours of the rocks that hem her in.

"The same tunnel?" she asks, because Kit seems to know everything. "Are you sure?"

"Unless you've moved since I last saw you."

The child's voice is growing weaker. It isn't fear she's hearing.

"Hold on. I'm going to try to come to you."

"Lily?"

"Yes?"

"...I'm sorry."

"You have nothing to be sorry for. This is not your fault."

Is that pained laughter? Or is it sobbing?

Lily digs her fingers into the spaces between the rocks.

The freshly fallen rocks are unstable. Lily is able to peel away small pebbles and roll a boulder far enough to create an opening through which fresh air pours in.

Fresh air. Fresh. The scent of the plains.

But by the time she squeezes herself through the opening, legs first, Kit has gone silent.

"Kit?" Lily's feet touch the sweet mercy of smooth stone on the other side. She slithers into standing.

"Stay with me!"

"It was my fault."

"What?"

"That they attacked us. I did that on purpose."

Lily pauses. Cannot quite process what she's hearing.

"I...what?"

"I wanted you to know, before..."

There is a skittering somewhere in the darkness, and then Lily is running in sheer terror, following the scent of open air.

She hits a wall and pinwheels wildly. Hits another. Finally calms herself enough to follow this wall, running fingers along the mandible-scarred rock, toward the source of the breeze.

"The good news *is*—" Kit is in pain, it's clear now. Terrible pain. "I think the collapse cut them off from us."

Small comforts. Lily still can't see any light.

"Kit, stay with me. It doesn't matter what you did."

"I am going to have to ask you to do something you'll hate."

Daylight. Shards of bright daylight, like a spiderweb crack in the Void.

"Lily?" The voice is in both ears, now. Lily scrambles toward it, then slows her pace. She imagines tripping and falling onto the injured child. Imagines Kit screaming in her ear.

She shuffles carefully along the rock wall, until her toe encounters soft flesh.

"Kit?"

"Thank the *gods*, Lily." The Eternal sounds near tears. Lily kneels and feels her way up Kit's body—

—to where it stops, just above the waist.

She feels at the rock wall that has half-buried the child. Their arms, shoulders, and head are beneath it.

"I'm going to dig you out."

"It was because my people—want this planet. We didn't know, didn't really understand. The raw materials, they told me it could grow *billions* of new brains for us—"

"Hush. Hush now." Lily does not want to hear this while she's trying to save the Eternal's life.

"Lily, I'm so *sorry*. If you had died—" Kit cannot finish.

"Shh. Shh. I didn't. And you're not going to either." The small stones come away easily from around Kit's chest and shoulders, but there's something larger, deeper down—

There is a boulder, too near where Kit's head should be. Lily feels her way down it with careful fingers, looking for the place where stone stops and flesh begins.

She finds Kit's hair, and freezes. The hair is slick. And the head beneath it…

Lily touches what can only be a skull fragment, and retches.

There is a smile in Kit's voice as they say: "I'm Graduating a little early."

Lily had no second soul. A similar blow to the head for her would have been final. And so, Kit explained, they could not, could not forgive themself for putting Lily in mortal danger. It could have been the end of her.

Lily is grateful for that. She is less grateful that the young Eternal keeps apologizing, all the way through the operation that simply feels like murder. Removing a warm, still-pulsing brain from a ruined skull is hard enough without the string of apologies that fade into silence.

She is as gentle as she can be. Kit assured her, before the end, that they felt no pain. No more than the rockfall had caused, and Lily could do nothing about that but end it. The brain itself has no pain receptors. It has no reason to. If something has penetrated the skull, it's already too late to run or hide.

Lily extracts Kit's second soul—a sheet of interconnected silicon chips embedded in the membrane over the brain—and leaves their body cooling. Cradles the silicon matrix like a precious artifact as she digs and kicks her way through the final wall of rubble.

She wonders, sometimes, what would have happened if the stone had hit the left side of Kit's head instead of the right. The Eternal's extra circuitry had left them with the ability to speak—but if their primary language center had been gone, if they could not talk Lily through the operation, what would have...?

Lily shakes her head at the thought of Kit's second soul languishing for centuries on the floor of an alien colony that no humanoid will set foot inside again.

It makes sense, in retrospect. By adding her DNA to the Queen's droplet, Lily added herself to the Ant's chemical vocabulary. To the list of things that were important, relevant. But she did not paint herself as family. There was nothing familiar about her.

She painted herself as a disease.

Such foreign DNA on the Queen's tongue meant one thing—infection. The carrier was to be destroyed, and anything chemically similar guarded against with savage force.

Kit had known this. Kit had known. They had led Lily out of Eden, considered her, for the span of a few hours, to be acceptable collateral damage.

But Kit had never seen anyone die before.

When the Ant turned on Lily, they realized the horror of their mistake. Grabbed Lily, *ran* with her toward the exit. They were close, so close, when...

"Thank the gods," Kit had said with a smile in their voice, as Lily peeled back pieces of her fractured skull, "that both of us survived."

"I will do something for you," Kit had promised, at the end. "I will do something for you, in return. Of course. Of course."

Lily hadn't cared. She had wanted to drag the Eternal whole from the rubble, bring them home and feed them in the garden. But she knew by the feel, by what she could imagine of the look of them, that they were dead no matter what she did.

That their *body* was dead, anyway.

It was strange to think of the flexible silicon sheet she carried in her hands as a living being. Without a power supply, Kit was effectively sleeping. But she cradled the chips like an idol, like a friend, until the Eternal elders came and took them from her.

Then she made her report to the Reshaped, and she waited.

Would there be war over this? Over the first attempt by an Eternal to infringe on Reshaped space? To infringe, more importantly, on the territory of a pre-technological *sentient* species, a defenseless species—unless Kit had lied about that too.

Would the Eternals begin to eliminate the Reshaped with the same neat efficiency Kit had shown in altering, then shedding, their own living body? Would the Reshaped begin developing defenses, ways to sound out hidden Eternals and blow them out of the sky?

Would she be reassigned, this world now a combat zone? Repairing the relationship between Ants and Earth life would take decades of experimentation. Decades spent creating a new kind of Reshaped person who could speak to the Ants in more eloquent and nuanced tones.

How does a virus convince its host that it is friendly? By demonstrating benign intelligence, maybe. And how does one demonstrate intelligence to a hivemind? That would become the question for the new Reshaped to answer.

The news came, mere days after Lily handed the chips to a tight-lipped Eternal over. Her own overs, symmetrical and perfect, called to speak with her from an open room in a paradisal forest.

"The Eternals tell us," they had said, "that you aided them

in gaining invaluable insights about the Ants of the Inanna mountain range. Well done."

Lily had blinked. What of her report of Kit's subversion? What of the Eternal's plot?

"It seems," the over continued, "that the Eternal who aided you has also been given special recognition."

Also?

"And they have used it to request jurisdiction over the Inanna system."

A pause. Lily waited.

"The Eternal 'Kit' has chosen geosynchronous orbit over your outpost as their location. The Eternals will not further develop this world. Instead, they plan to use it as a source of information. Information from us. Which you will relay to them. They believe that new algorithms will be generated through the study of Inanna's native life."

'I will do something for you...'

"We will be sending your first cohort of assistants within three standard months. I hope that twelve will be enough."

Twelve...not replacements, but *assistants*?

"The Eternal Kit also states that they will be beaming instructions to your chemical synthesizers, and to our scientists. Instructions for an apology, and a formal introduction to the people of Inanna."

'People!'

"They believe that your collaboration will prove fruitful. So do we."

Lily had shuddered to see Kit's new "body"—a Voidlike blackness, a hole in the bright lights of their creche. Camouflage and safety, that body was—they would be able to pass millennia unnoticed, pass within centimeters of a Reshaped ship in safety, their sensors collecting data and solid-state processors grasping at the questions of Eternity.

Lily does not fully understand, even, what those questions are. Hers are the questions of flesh and bone and blood.

And her questions, Kit has told her through their earlink, are important also. Kit speaks rarely, now, becoming less animal and more Eternal with each passing day. But Lily uploads her team's data faithfully, every night. She will for the rest of her life.

Lily still looks up and speaks to the stars at night.

But now she knows one of them is listening.

LIKE THIS BOOK?

Your review GoodReads.com review helps others who might like the book find it, too. This can help the author and publisher release more books!

You can leave a review here:
Review on GoodReads.com

You can also sign up for the author's mailing list here:
Sign Up for C. L. Kagmi's Mailing List

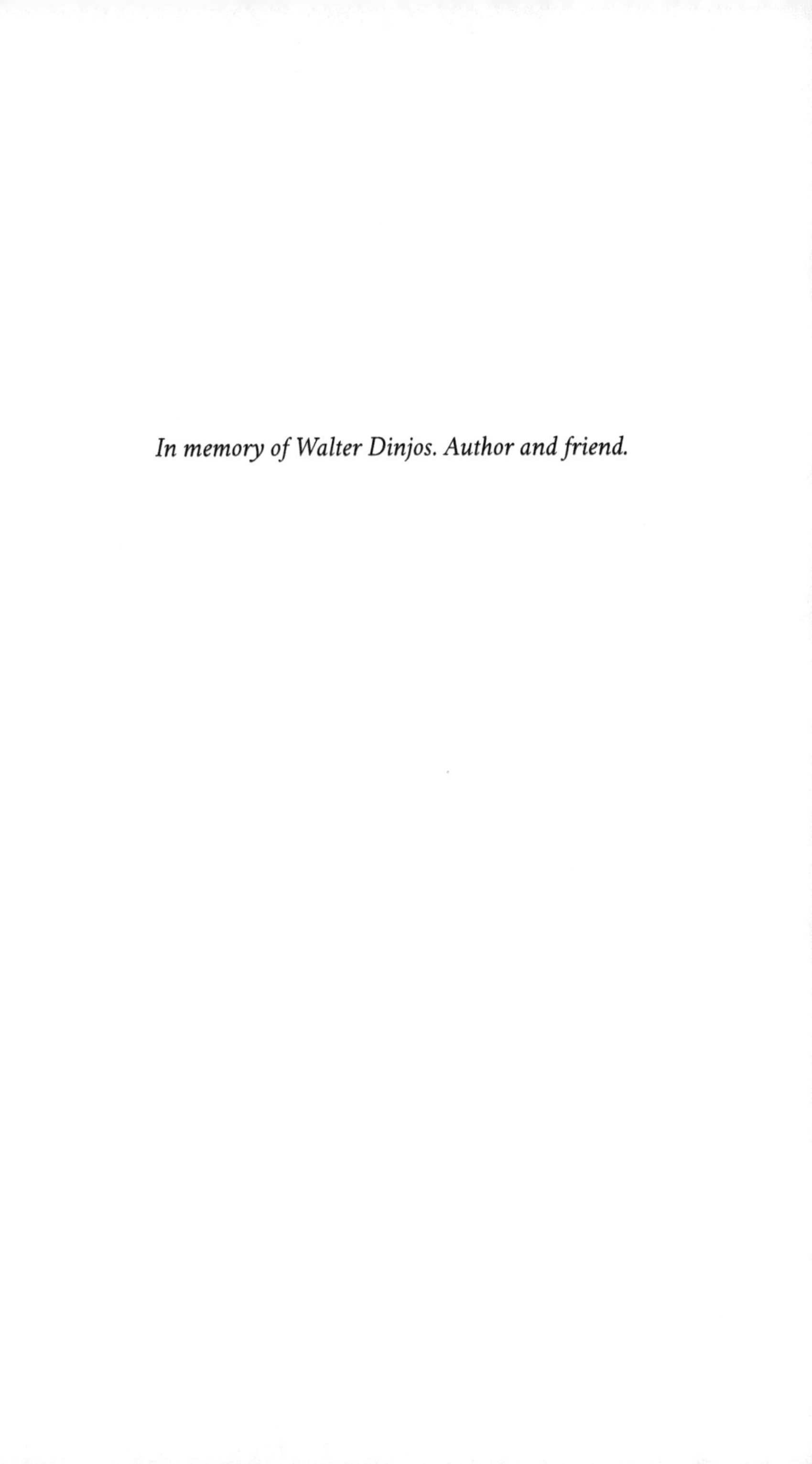

In memory of Walter Dinjos. Author and friend.

In Memoriam: Walter Dinjos

The late Walter Dinjos wrote truly remarkable science fiction and fantasy, steeped in Nigerian culture and musical poetry. We were once collaborators on plans to cross-advertise our short stories before his sudden and totally unexpected death.

His writing career ended far too soon, but his works can still be read as Kindle singles through his Amazon author page (QR code below), or in the publications in which they originally appeared (listed below):

The Woodcutter's Deity, *Writers of the Future Vol. 33*
The Mama Mmri, *Best of Beneath Ceaseless Skies Vol. 8*
A Hundred Lifetimes, *Deep Magic, December 2016*
Being a Giant in Men's World, *Galaxy's Edge, May 2018*
The Worst Breed of Vultures, *Bourbon Penn Vol. 12*
The Diamond Fish, *Myriad Lands Issue 1; available as Kindle single.*
Sing Me A Song, *LampLight Vol. 5, Issue 1; available as Kindle single.*
Irony So Efficient, *James Gunn's Ad Astra*

ACKNOWLEDGMENTS

All books are the work of many hands. I've been dreaming and woolgathering and cross-pollinating for years, but this book would not be what it is without the support and assistance of many people.

I would of course like to thank my parents, including author Mary Marshall, who managed to instill in me a passion for storytelling and a love of weird fiction from an early age. Thanks also to my mentor and life coach, Colleen McGee, for helping me to take a no-nonsense approach to the business side of my writing career.

Thanks to my dearest Twila, my writer brothers Andrew L. Roberts and Doug C. Souza, my most relentless fan C. T. Silver, and the wonderful Cliff Winnig for their sometimes forceful encouragement to get this manuscript to the presses. I will take this opportunity to make a shameless plug in favor of Roberts' recently released book "Duramen Rose," which I believe is one of the finest texts available today for learning about the reality of war.

Writers of the Future judges Robert J. Sawyer, David

Farland, and Tim Powers have been instrumental in convincing me that stories can change lives and that this work is worth doing. The speculative fiction community as a whole owes them a great debt for the generous support and teaching they've offered to dozens of new authors over the years.

I also owe a great debt to Joe Stech, who bought the first story I ever sold for *Compelling Science Fiction* and who helped bring my work to wider audiences. His enthusiasm over "Skychildren" years later was also a gift, especially when he checked the math on some of my worldbuilding physics.

Tremendous thanks to Bảo Lã and Long Nyugẽn for reaching out to me to initiate the translation of "Skychildren" and "Twiceborn" for Vietnamese-speaking readers, and to Sean Patrick Hazlett for arranging the publication of my short story "Evangeline" in 2020 Baen Books anthology *Weird World War III*.

"Evangeline" isn't in this book, her publication helped encourage me to move forward with publishing this collection. She can be found in Baen's wonderfully strange tome about what might have happened if the Cold War had gone *weird*.

Thanks to Jamie Wahls, Julianne Angeli, and the late Walter Dinjos for their thoughtful and sensitive feedback on my previously unpublished works. I believe I've benefited tremendously from their wonderfully diverse feedback.

Special honors are due to Michael Michera, who won the Golden Brush Award for the beautiful illustration that accompanied "The Drake Equation" in *Writers of the Future Vol. 33* and who generously agreed to allow me to offer a version of this art to purchasers of this book.

Thanks to the good folks at Teaologie Tea Company for keeping me fueled.

And lastly, thanks for the encouragement of oathkeeper Jesse Kulla, who is authorized to make really, really sure I make my publication deadline.

Copyright © 2021 by Stella Luma

"After the Upload" © 2015 by C. L. Kagmi

"Sheanna" © 2015 by C. L. Kagmi

"Twiceborn" © 2016 by C. L. Kagmi

"The Drake Equation" © 2016 by C. L. Kagmi

"On Speaking With The Stars" © 2017 by C. L. Kagmi

"Skychildren" © 2017 by C. L. Kagmi

https://clkagmi.com/contact/

Quantity sales. Special discounts are available on quantity purchases by bookstores, corporations, associations, and others. For details, contact the publisher at the address above.

Paperback ISBN: 979-8-9850761-0-3

Ebook ISBN: 979-8-9850761-1-0

ABOUT THE AUTHOR

 C. L. Kagmi is an inveterate wanderer who splits her time between the American Midwest and West Coast. She likes any surprise that doesn't end in grievous bodily injury. Don't test her on that, though, as she has a firm grip and has been known to bite.

She earned her B.S. in Neuroscience from the University of Michigan in 2011 and worked in emergency medicine research for five years before becoming a full-time freelance writer. Today she offers ghostwriting and writing coaching services. She has assisted in the production and publication of dozens of books and articles for business and tech publications.

Her work has appeared in *Analog Science Fiction & Fact*, *Compelling Science Fiction*, *SFVN*, and *Writers of the Future Vol. 33*.

CLKagmi.com
Facebook.com/CLKagmi
Twitter.com/CLKagmi